Obsessed with my Wife's Best Friend 3

By Lady Lissa & Shelli Marie

Recap from book 2

Tangi

Waking up in Smooth's bed that next morning was everything. Yes, it was a bold move to just show up at his place and let myself in, but I was desperate. All I could do was lay there and stare at his handsome face as he slept.

Finally facing reality, I knew that it was only a matter of time before my secret affair with Dallas was out. I had to start planning.

What I really needed was Smooth. Reason being, I had to have my allies outnumber my enemies and right then, things weren't looking so good for the home team. Even Dallas was on my bad side.

Of course, I had Tierra for the moment, but I couldn't run to her. She had her own life. Her own happiness. Now it was my turn and I was gonna get my fairytale ending too, even if I had to do unthinkable things to ensure it!

"I love you." I chanted as I kissed Smooth's lips. He slowly opened one eye and started laughing before hugging me tightly.

"I love you too baby, but you really need to talk to Tierra. That's the only way you're gonna get past all this. You're over here having breakdowns and fighting with that nigga Dallas. Hell, you got me and your brother beating his ass, risking our freedom and all this can be resolved by you confessing your wrongs to Tierra. You yourself admitted that shit Tangi. Just tell her baby and let's get on with our lives. Don't you miss this shit? Don't you miss me?"

I stood there not saying a word. That shit right there said it all...

Smooth got up and started gathering all my stuff, including the boxes that I was going through last night. He was quiet the whole time. He didn't speak until he had everything packed up neatly by his bedroom door.

"Where's your keys so I can put this shit in your car. I don't want you to have no excuses for just dropping by like that again," he said with a nasty attitude. "Oh, and please be dressed and ready to go by the time I'm finished."

Like what the fuck was really going on? What kind of shit was that? First, we made love all day and night, and now he was throwing me out of his house like I was some random bitch.

Smooth could be a cold muthafucka when he wanted to be. I hated that shit, but it turned me the fuck on too.

But I knew right then wasn't the time to push it. Like he said, I got my ass up and put my clothes on. I wasn't about to allow him to play me anymore than he already had.

To save face, I carried the last box to the garage before Smooth could make it back inside to get it. "Okay, this is it. I guess I'm gone." I said trying to sound just as sad as I felt. I didn't want to leave. I wanted to stand there and demand that he love me for me! I just wanted him to forget the confession I made. I just wanted him to tell me that he loved me enough to see past my faults and shit. But it didn't seem like he was going to do it though.

"Aight then," Smooth chanted out as he opened the garage door. That was my cue to get in my car and get going.

I really wanted to go off, but I couldn't do that. I was already hurting like crazy. The last thing I wanted was for him to see me cry again. Sadly driving away, I looked in the rearview mirror and watched the garage door go down and the image of Smooth disappear. Now it was official. I had really lost him forever.

The irony of that statement caused me to pull over to the side of the road. I started crying harder than I cried before because at least before, there was a little hope for he and I to rekindle what we had. But Smooth was still on that bullshit about me telling Tierra the truth. It was like he wasn't even hearing me or listening to the reasons why I couldn't tell her.

How the hell could I tell Tierra some shit like that? She meant everything to me right now. As selfish as that may sound, I couldn't tell Tierra about what I had done because I didn't want to lose her. She was all I had. I tried praying to God for peace, but of course he wouldn't give it to me. How could I get peace when I was hiding such a huge secret from my best friend? Everything in me was telling me to confess, but I just couldn't do it. I knew in my heart that she'd never be able to forgive me for betraying her that way.

There was only one thing that I could do to get him back, but I was truly terrified. How could I tell Tierra?

Being torn behind it all, I did what I knew best to do. I went home and drank until I passed out.

Waking up hours later, I heard my cell going off. I didn't know where it was, so I had to follow the nonstop ringing.

"Hello?"

"Tangi?! I've been calling you since last night. What is going on with you? Are you alright?" Tierra hollered out like I was hard of hearing.

"Nothing, I'm okay," I lied. She just had a baby, so there was no reason to stress her out about anything going on with me. It wasn't as if I could really tell her what was going on anyway. "It's just that I was with Smooth trying to work things out and..."

"Girl I hope that goes well and all but let me tell you about Dallas just stopping by here..."

Just like it had been lately, Tierra was going on and on about what she was going through, it only reminded me that it was all because of me. Everything that she had going on was my fault. She and Dallas were happy until I started messing with him. They weren't happy happy, but they were happy enough. I felt like shit for taking that away from her.

Ready to tell her everything, I reached over and grabbed my bottle of Jack off the table. Oh yeah, a bitch was ready to get really bold. I would've too... if my cell wouldn't have suddenly died.

"Oh, well, I guess this wasn't the right time!" I laughed and cried all at the same damn time.

Then it was right back to the bottle...

Two days later I was finally done with my drinking binge. It was time to clean myself up and pull it together. I needed something in my life to make me smile again. The first person that came to mind was Tierra.

Throwing on my shoes, I decided to go over to Tierra's to see how she and the baby were doing. She had called me because Thaddeus had some business to handle at the gym, so she wanted me to keep her company. I was more than happy to go over there and spend time with Miracle. Hopefully, that would take my mind off of everything that was going on between me and Smooth.

I arrived at her house half an hour later. Thaddeus left soon afterward. Tierra was feeding the baby when I got there. She was just a natural at being a mom. That was so cute. I couldn't help but think about my baby that I "lost." But I had to remember that this wasn't about me. This was about spending time with my goddaughter and bestie.

After she finished feeding Miracle, she burped her and changed her diaper.

"Would you like to hold her?" Tierra asked.

"I'd love to," I said with a smile.

Tierra had been home for two weeks with her baby girl. She didn't want to leave Miracle's side since she was premature and had breathing issues at the hospital. She had a small oxygen tank to keep handy just in case anything went wrong. But up until then, everything had been good. Thank God!

"I see she's gained weight!" I teased.

"Yes, with her lil greedy butt! She weighs five pounds and four ounces now! She wants to nurse every five minutes and shit... my boobs are on swole!" she frowned rubbing her now size 'D' breasts. Tierra handed the baby to me and I smiled at her little miracle baby.

"Tierra, she's so beautiful!" I gushed.

"Thank you. I'm so glad I got to bring her home. Them folks was crazy thinking that I was gonna leave her at the hospital. But I knew it! Miracle got stronger because she is a fighter like her mommy!"

"Yes, she is! Looking just like you too Tierra!"

I could see the love she had for her baby in her eyes. She had wanted this for so long. Thank God for her 'Miracle' because that was what she truly was! How could I be envious of that?

"Have you heard from your soon to be ex?" I brought up to cut the awkward silence.

"Not since that day he popped his ass up over here! Girl he is ridiculous! I don't know what I ever saw in him," she said.

"Are you going to let him be involved in Miracle's life?" I asked.

"I wish I could say hell no, but he is her father..."

"The father that wanted you to terminate your pregnancy!" I finished. Dallas didn't deserve to be in this baby's life. The fact that he wanted Tierra to have an abortion spoke volumes about what kind of father he would be.

"Yea, I know, but now that she's here, he feels differently. You should've seen the look on his face when he first laid eyes on her. It almost made me feel bad to throw his ass out," she said.

"So, you really think he would benefit being in your baby's life?"

"That's really not my decision to make Tangi. If he takes me to court, a judge could easily grant him visitation. I mean, what legit reason would I have for keeping him from her? Because he cheated on me with some bitch? Because he left me? Because he told me to terminate my pregnancy? The judge could say that he's changed his feelings toward the baby now and our personal issues have nothing to do with whether he'd be a good father to Miracle or not," she explained. "At the end of the day, I'm not trying to get into a custody battle with him. When Miracle gets a little stronger, I'm gonna allow him to visit with her. After all, he is her father."

I knew she was trying to make the right decision for her and her daughter, but I didn't think it was right. I didn't think that Dallas deserved to be in this baby's life. She was too young to know what a devil he really was.

I wanted to try and talk Tierra out of her decision, but I didn't. I couldn't chance her getting suspicious.

"I understand. Your baby is just so precious. I hope he doesn't do anything to..."

"Don't say it! I'm having a hard enough time trying to do the right thing as it is." Miracle fell asleep in my arms. "I'm gonna go put her in her crib. The last thing I want is for her little butt to get spoiled."

After kissing Miracle on the forehead, I handed her over to Tierra. When I drew back, I heard my phone ringing. It had been doing so for the past few minutes, but I didn't want to answer it because I was enjoying holding the baby. Now that Tierra had taken her to put her in bed, I pulled the phone out. Looking at it, I saw that it was Smooth calling.

I wondered what he wanted. I mean, he had made shit very clear that he didn't want anything to do with me until I told Tierra the truth. So, why was he calling me now? I heard Tierra singing and humming to her baby, so I stepped outside to call Smooth back.

"Hey, you busy?" he asked.

"What can I do for you? Did I forget something at your house?" I asked.

"No, I just needed to talk to you about something."

"About what? I thought you said everything you needed to say when we saw each other."

"Tangi, you believe me when I say I love you right?"

"Look, I'm not trying to hear all that right now. You keep saying you love me, fuck me, and then leave or put me out. I mean, you already told me how you feel, and I told you how I feel. It seems as if we're at an impasse."

"Look baby, I know that you're scared to talk to Tierra. I understand how you feel. I know that shit is hard for you. That's why I'm offering to go with you when you tell her."

"What?"

What the hell was he talking about?

"I love you Tangi. I wanna marry you, so I'm offering to be your support system when you tell Tierra the truth. Maybe she'll take it better if she sees that I know and I'm still with you. It might be hard for her to hear at first, but as close as the two of you are, I have a strong feeling that sooner or later, she'll come around." Smooth reasoned like he just all of a sudden had the perfect solution. Shit, all I could picture was the same outcome. All bad!

I didn't understand why he couldn't just leave that shit alone. I loved him, but I loved Tierra also. Tierra and I had been through so much together. We had been through a lot of ups and downs, and our friendship remained strong over the years. This was something I knew that she would never forgive me for. I knew if I told her that would be the end of our friendship, and I couldn't risk that. She needed me just as much as I needed her.

"Look Smooth, I love you. Shit, I love you a lot. But if our relationship is contingent on me telling Tierra the truth about me and Dallas, I'm just gonna have to say goodbye to you forever..."

"Really? You're really just gonna end things with us like that?"

"I'm not ending things with us... you are! You're the one who won't just leave shit alone. I keep telling you that I'm not gonna do it. I can't do it. That shit would probably be easy for you to confess to one of your bros, but for me it's too hard. Tierra is one of the most important people in my life."

"That's why she deserves to know the truth!" he argued.

"Hell no! She doesn't deserve to know that shit! Don't you think I regret sleeping with Dallas and ruining their fuckin' marriage? Don't you think if I could do the shit over again, I'd do things differently..."

Suddenly I was cut off midsentence. Only Smooth wasn't the one interrupting me!

"What the fuck did you just say?" Tierra belted out behind me with so much venom in her tone that I could feel her poison.

Just the sound of her voice had me ready to piss on myself right then. I didn't even wanna turn to look at her because I knew she probably had nothing but hatred in her eyes. My heart literally plummeted to my stomach. Tears sprang to my eyes almost immediately because I knew this wasn't going to end well.

Dammit!

"I gotta go!" I said to Smooth as I hung the phone up in his face and put it away. I wanted to pretend that I didn't hear her, but when I heard her taking steps behind me, I knew that wasn't going to be possible.

"Tangi, I know you hear me talking to you!" When I still didn't respond or turn to face her, she grabbed me by the shoulder and roughly turned me around. "It was you?"

"It was me what?"

"Bitch don't fuckin' play with me... not right now!"

Damn! She called me a bitch, so obviously she overheard something.

"Tierra, I..."

"Please tell me that I did not hear what I thought I just heard," she said as she locked eyes with me. Tears were brimming from her eyes, but she patted them away.

"Tierra..." I couldn't even look her in the eyes.

"Don't Tierra me! All this time I've been wondering who was messing with my husband... and it was you. You're the bitch who was sleeping with my husband? Please tell me I heard you wrong because I know yo' ass ain't that fuckin' low!"

Now our eyes were locked and the only thing in my view was the hurtful expression that Tierra wore. Tears overflowed from her eyes and right then I knew. I knew that there was no more running.

It was now time for me to face the truth. In my case like most, with the truth came the shit and it was all about to hit the fan...

Chapter One

Tierra

I returned to the living room to find Tangi missing. I called her name a couple of times, but she didn't respond to me. I heard her voice coming from outside, so I went to find her. As I got closer to the door, it sounded as if she was a little aggravated. I bet that she was talking to Smooth. I was about to tell her to hang up on his ass. I wasn't sure why they had broken up, but she was too pretty and had too much going for herself to be begging any man to take her back. However, that wasn't even the basis of their conversation. It seemed as though I was the topic of discussion and the next statement she made, sent a chill running up my spine.

"Hell no! She doesn't deserve to know that shit! Don't you think I regret sleeping with Dallas and ruining their fuckin' marriage? Don't you think if I could do the shit over again, I'd do things differently..." I heard Tangi saying.

I almost lost my footing hearing her say that. My mouth went dry and my head even started spinning. Was something wrong with my hearing? I mean, I had to have misunderstood what she had just said. I mean,

Tangi wasn't just my best friend, but she was like a sister to me. She was closer to me than anyone else in this world, so you could imagine how hurt I was when I heard those words spoken from her mouth.

Was she really saying that she was the reason my marriage to Dallas fell apart? Was she really standing there talking to someone about sleeping with my ex... knowing how it had made me feel? I literally had spoken to Tangi about every single thing in my marriage to Dallas. I spoke to her about how good he made me feel when we had sex. I spoke to her about how much I loved him. And I even spoke to her when I found out he was cheating on me. Hell, I had asked her to help me find the woman he had been cheating on me with... and the whole time it was her.

As I approached her, my legs grew shaky. This was my best friend in the whole wide world. Surely, she couldn't be serious about having ruined my marriage by sleeping with Dallas. I waited for her to face me once I made my presence known, but she didn't, so I flung her around so she could look at me. I just needed her to tell me that I had heard her wrong or misunderstood what I heard.

"Tierra please..." she begged with tears in her eyes.

"Tangi, I know what I heard. I just wanna know why you would do something like that to me. Haven't I always been there for you?"

"Yes."

"What would make you do me like that?"

"Tierra..."

"I want you to stop CALLING MY FUCKING NAME!!" I yelled growing frustrated. I took a deep breath and tried to calm my nerves down before I continued. "You and I both know my name is Tierra. Now, answer the question. Why?"

"I'm so sorry. I didn't mean for you to find out this way..."

"Of course, you didn't. From the way you sounded on the phone, you didn't intend for me to ever find out!"

"It was a mistake and I'm sorry!"

"A MISTAKE?! IT WAS A MISTAKE?! YOU BUSTED UP MY MARRIAGE BY SLEEPING WITH MY HUSBAND AND YOU CALL IT A MISTAKE?!!" I yelled. The fact that she would stand there telling me that shit had me furious.

"Tierra..."

WHAP!

That was the first time I had ever struck Tangi in my life. I never thought that I'd ever have a reason to do something like that to her, but she deserved it. She was lucky that I was still recovering from that C-section, otherwise, I'd drag her ass up and down this damn driveway. She held her left cheek with her mouth open as tears spilled from her eyes.

"This whole time I've been telling you that I suspected Dallas was cheating on me! This whole time I had you in my house smelling his draws! This whole time I had been confiding in you! And this whole time, you were the bitch that I was complaining about!" I said as I wiped my tears away. "I bet you and Dallas had some good laughs about my blind ass huh?"

"It wasn't like that," she cried.

"Oh no?! Well, please tell me what it was like. I thought you loved me..."

"I do love you Tierra... that's why I never wanted you to find out!"

"Bitch if you hadn't fucked my husband, there wouldn't be shit for me to find out! You betrayed me in the worst possible way with yo triflin' ass!" I snapped as I looked her up and down. "I can't believe that you did that shit to me."

"I never meant for that to happen. It just did..."

WHAP!

That's right, I slapped her ass again. She and I had been best friends since elementary. We shared so many bonding and close moments that sisters probably never shared. She was the maid of honor at my wedding. She was going to be my daughter's godmother. She was the person I confided in about everything. So, for her to tell me that sleeping with Dallas just happened... that bitch was lying like a rug! She let that shit happen!

"DON'T YOU EVER SAY THAT SHIT TO ME! YOU AND DALLAS MADE A CONSCIOUS DECISION TO FUCK EACH OTHER BEHIND MY BACK! THAT SHIT DIDN'T JUST HAPPEN!!" I yelled as I pointed my finger in her face, nudging her in the forehead.

"I'm so sorry..."

I raised my hand with my palm facing her mouth because I didn't need her to apologize anymore. She had broken my heart and there was no coming back from that. The woman who stood before me wasn't the same person I cherished from back in the day. That person would've never hurt me this way. I felt as if my soul had been crushed. I could literally hear my heart breaking in my chest. It sounded like glass breaking.

"I don't need you to ever apologize to me again. You went too far Tangi, and we can never get back what we once had..."

She shook her head from side to side as tears streamed from her eyes. "Please don't say that. We can fix..."

"We can't fix shit! You fucked my husband! That night he was calling me T and shit, telling me about some damn trick I do with my tongue... he was talking about yo grimy ass!" I reflected back on that night my husband literally choked me with his dick trying to get me to do the shit she was used to doing to him. "UGH! You disgust me!"

"I love you Tierra! Please..."

"I hate you!" I spewed at her.

"Please don't say that. You're just upset..."

"Don't try to tell me how I fucking feel! I HATE YOU!!" I hollered again so she would know that I was dead ass serious. "I never want to see you again!"

"But what about the baby?"

"What about her?"

"I thought you wanted me to be her godmother..."

"Bitch I hope you got a good look at her because that was the last time you will ever see my baby again!"

"Tierra please don't do this!"

"I didn't do shit! You and Dallas did it all!" I reminded as I mean mugged her. "Now, get the fuck off my damn property!"

"Please... we've been friends for way too long to let that nigga come between us!"

Oh, no she didn't! Even if I could get past what she and Dallas did, our friendship was over. I'd never be able to trust Tangi again... EVER!! She had made sure of that shit by committing the ultimate betrayal against our friendship. I thought that we were too close for anything like that to ever happen. I never looked at a man that she dated in that way. I would've never crossed that line between us because I loved her too much. Obviously, I respected our friendship way more than she did.

"That nigga didn't come between us! You broke us apart! For that, I'll never be able to forgive or trust you!" I said. "Now, I'm gonna tell you one last time... GET THE FUCK OFF MY PROPERTY!!"

"I love you Tierra..." she said with tears in her eyes.

"GOOOOOOOOO!!" I yelled.

Before she could say anything else, I turned and went into my house. I closed the door then spotted her purse on the table. I walked over to it and snatched it up. I opened the door and threw her shit to the ground. I slammed my door as she banged on it.

"TIERRA PLEASE!!" she cried.

BANG! BANG! BANG!

"TIERRRRRRA!! I'M SORRY!!"

Fuck that bitch!

I slid my back down the door until my butt hit the floor. I couldn't believe that she had done that to me. Tears burned as they fell from my eyes behind our broken friendship. Tangi and I would never be friends again. We'd never speak again. We'd never be shit again. I thought slapping her those couple of times would help me feel better, but it only made me feel worst. I sat on the floor crying and grieving over the loss of our friendship and sisterhood. Never in my life had I imagined our friendship ending this way or for that reason.

Friends were supposed to cherish each other, not stab them in the back. What Tangi had done to us was the most horrible shit she could've done. All the dreams for our future had now dissipated. She had put a nail in the coffin and there was no removing it. I hope that it was all worth it to her. I truly hope that she and Dallas were happy about this.

Tangi had destroyed our friendship just like Dallas had destroyed our marriage. Neither of them deserved any kind of forgiveness. But damn, why did this shit have to hurt so much? I felt more pain losing Tangi than I did when I lost Dallas. I guess it was because I had Tangi to lean on for support. Now, I had neither one of them.

As I clutched my chest from the overwhelming sense of heartache, I just laid on the floor. I couldn't believe this had happened.

Lord give me the strength I need to get through this...

Chapter Two

Tangi

How I felt when I heard Tierra's voice was something I couldn't even describe. I just knew that my whole entire world was going to be different. Tierra and I had never gotten in any arguments or fights, so for her to hit me not only once, but twice... I knew that her feelings were extremely hurt. "Tierra please let me explain!" I cried as I knocked on her door.

I couldn't lose my best friend. She was all I had in the world.

Ring... buzz, ring...

My phone started ringing and I checked it. It was Smooth. Oh, I couldn't wait to speak to his ass. If it wasn't for him, none of this would be happening. All I wanted was for him to either respect my decision or leave me alone.

"What do you want?!" I asked with an attitude as I got in my car and headed home.

"Are you okay?"

"No, I'm not okay. I may never be okay again!" I fumed.

"What's wrong? Do you need me to meet up with you?"

"I need you to leave me alone!" I shot harshly.

"What? What did I do?"

"Because of your constant badgering to tell Tierra the truth, she overheard me talking to you..."

"Oh wow! So, she knows?"

"Yes, she knows. Now, she won't talk to me! She says our friendship is over and I can't be Miracle's godmother! Are you happy now? Huh Smooth? Are you happy that I lost my best friend?" I asked angrily.

"Of course I'm not happy Tangi, but you should've known that would happen once she found out," he said.

"You're right! I knew that's exactly what would happen... that's why I didn't wanna tell her! But you kept pestering me to say something to her, and now she knows!" I cried as the warm salty liquid rained from my eyes down into my mouth.

"Tangi, I'm so sorry. Do you want me to come meet you?"

"You're kidding right?"

"No. I know how hurt you are, so I'd like to be there for you."

"I don't want you nowhere near me Smooth..."

"What? You're blaming this on me?"

"You damn skippy! If you would've left well enough alone, I would still have my best friend! She would've never found out about me and Dallas if it wasn't for you!"

"Tangi, now I know you're upset and all, but surely, you have to take some of that blame. I mean, if you hadn't done the deed, you wouldn't have lost Tierra. You and Dallas are the ones who fucked over your friend. Shit, I was just trying to get you to free yourself of that burden!"

My heart was so hurt right now. I not only lost my best friend, but I lost my goddaughter too. If I had known Smooth was calling about that same bullshit, I would've never called his ass back. Like, why couldn't he have stayed out of it and mind his fucking business. The way he was acting, you would've thought that Tierra was related to him or something.

"IT WAS MY BURDEN TO CARRY... NOT YOURS!! I wish I had never told you my secret, but I knew if I didn't Dallas would. I just wanted to come clean with you before he did thinking that we'd be okay. But then you got all righteous and holier than thou wanting me to confess to Tierra. Why couldn't you have just left it alone?!" I asked as I broke down crying again.

"I won't let you blame me for your issues!"

"You ain't gotta let me do shit! Just leave me alone. You've done enough to fuck up my life!" I huffed before I ended the call.

Whether Smooth wanted to admit it or not, he had a hand in what happened today. He kept pressuring me to come clean with Tierra when I had told him time and time again that wasn't something I wanted to do. Now, everything was ruined.

The damage was done and all that was left for me to do was go home and sulk. No one was going to feel sorry for me, but myself.

Once in the privacy of my home a half hour later, I peeled out of my clothes and poured a stiff drink while I reflected on my day. Taking my triple shot of whiskey into my bedroom, I sat on my bed in nothing except my black bra and panty set.

After finishing that drink, my mind was cloudy, my head was spinning and Smooth was beating at my door. That was the last thing I needed.

He can't come in! I'm not ready to see anyone! I don't deserve to see anyone!

Stumbling off the bed, I ran around cutting all the lights off and drawing all the blinds closed. Smooth was banging on the door and buzzing my cell nonstop the entire time.

Ready to ignore the world, I ran back to my bedroom, locked myself in, then shoved my phone into the bottom of my handbag and threw it into my closet. Swiftly shuffling my bare feet through the soft carpeting, I climbed onto the middle of my bed and curled up in the fetal position.

Lifting the sheet partially over my head, I closed my eyes and began rocking my body back and forth. The swaying was soothing, but after about 60 seconds of it, my stomach began to turn.

Vomit was threatening to spew out, but I held that shit in and forced myself to sleep. Just like before, I stayed in a drunken state for the next four to five days. All I did was eat, drink, throw up, sleep then repeat.

On the sixth day, Smooth sent the fucking white folks over to do a welfare check on me! I poked my head out of the door and asked, "Is this alive enough for you?"

The smell of the liquor spewing from my mouth probably singed the eyelashes off that red headed bitch. I knew the stench offended her by the way she turned her nose up.

"Bitch bye!" I told her before slamming the door in her face.

That visit was a wakeup call. Judging from the looks on their faces, I knew I looked a hot fucking mess. As I stood in the bedroom mirror, I was disgusted with what

I saw and the smell coming from my body made my own nose want to take a vacation. I smelled like shit and ass! I had never been this foul before in my life.

I really need to go wash my ass!

I was stinking from head to toe, literally! I'm saying my hair was funky, my breath was humming, my armpits were musty, my twat and ass were foul, and my feet were even tart! Nah, I was out of line and disrespecting myself with my odor!

Thoroughly disgusted with my outside appearance as well as my inside demons, I went into the bathroom praying as I stepped into the shower. Lathering and scrubbing my body over a good 20 times, I chanted the serenity prayer repeatedly.

As I got out, dried myself off and got dressed, I went to plug my cell in. Before it could begin chiming with alerts, I traveled to the kitchen to make me a veggie omelet.

First, I gotta clean this shit up!

Starting with the dishes, I tackled the entire mess within 20 minutes. The only thing left to do was take out the trash which smelled just as rotten as I had before I hopped in the shower.

Not thinking anything of it, I took hold of a bag in each hand and went out the side door where the cans were.

Roof, roof, roof!

The dogs next door began barking loudly, scaring the shit out of me! I thought they were after me, until I realized the fence was separating us.

Tossing the bags into the garbage receptacle, I swiveled around to face Jay. I didn't even hear him creep up on me.

"Why the fuck you didn't just come through the front door Jay?! It ain't like you don't have a key!" I reminded as I rolled my eyes and went back inside the house.

Following me into the kitchen, my brother started in on all this shit with Dallas. Of course, Smooth had already told him what happened. Jay just wanted to hear my version. Instead of complaining and whining, I told him that whatever Smooth said was what happened. That cut that conversation real short!

"So, are you cool, sis?" Jay inquired with a funny look before he busted out in a smile.

"Yeah, you know me."

"I do know you. That's exactly why I'm asking. Seriously though, are you good?" he pressed with a concerned grin. "I mean, I know how much Tierra means to you. That falling out between y'all has gotta be hard."

"It is, but I can't do shit about it. She won't even talk to me, so forgiveness is definitely out of the question at this point. I'll be just fine, but I'm not gonna be helping down at the club though. I don't even wanna see Smooth let alone work around him..."

"I knew that shit was coming. That's why I planned a little something for you."

"What Jay?" I sighed with absolutely no enthusiasm whatsoever.

"I own a timeshare in Oregon, but I took it off the rental app for a couple of months. Go out there and chill. It's up by Mount Hood so the view is great..."

"No thanks..."

"Why not? You need to get away from all this drama you've been going through, and that would be the perfect place for you to retreat," he offered.

"It's gonna be cold as fuck out there!"

"Well, you don't have to go. However, if you change your mind, here's all the info and a set of keys to the property." Jay explained as he pulled a manila envelope from his inside pocket and handed it to me.

Checking out the contents, my attention was immediately captured by the property brochure with all the details. I instantly fell in love with the newly built home. It was in a remote location, but not that far from the grocery store and gas station. Maybe my brother was right. Maybe a change of scenery was exactly what I needed. Leave it to him to always have my back.

"I'll go, but I don't know how long I'll stay!" I smiled and gave my brother a hug before walking him to the door. "I guess I'll have to book a flight..."

Holding his finger up, Jay got on his cell. "Give it a couple of minutes. You should get your airline reservation information in your Gmail account. You'll leave tomorrow on a night owl flight. I'm not driving to work that night, so you'll have to pick me up once the club closes..."

"Oh, you just knew I was gonna go!"

"Trust me sis, I really didn't! I just hoped that you would go, but if you're not ready that roundtrip ticket is flexible!"

Thanking my brother once again, I closed the door behind him and began packing two suitcases. I was about to do what I did best... run from my problems!

Dallas wasn't trying to let me leave in peace either because as soon as I closed my final bag that night, he was calling me back to back. I had changed my number several times, and every time he found out the new number. Shaking my head, I went ahead and answered it.

"Tangi! Where are you?! Haven't you gotten any of my fuckin' messages?! Why the fuck didn't you give me a heads up that you told Tierra..."

"Look you dirty muthafucka! Ugh!" I grunted as I gathered my words. "I didn't tell her shit, but she knows and now we have to deal with it!"

"She had me served with papers! She's seeking full custody and supervised visitations with Miracle!" Dallas complained harshly. "And tell me this Tangi... why the fuck these papers say that you're gonna testify that we had an affair and that I was stalking you and doing crazy shit! What type of shit did you tell her Tangi?! You really hate me enough to stop me from seeing my daughter?! You know I haven't seen her but twice since she was born?! I only held her..."

I let Dallas say everything he needed to then I cussed his ass out and told him that he was the sickest most selfish person I knew. All he was concerned about was his needs and wants. Like didn't he realize that I had lost my best friend in the world behind that shit with him?! Yet all he could do was complain about how shit wasn't going his way. I literally wanted to scream. I was so over him. I couldn't believe at one time I thought I was in love with his shady ass.

"We both made our beds Dallas. I'm adjusting to sleeping in mine and I suggest you do the same!"

"We need to be sleeping together Tangi! We need to stick together on this shit! Fuck Tierra and fuck that nigga Smooth! Help me get joint custody of Miracle and we can both be in her life! Tierra can't keep her from us if we work together!"

"Are you fuckin' crazy? Do you hear what you're saying Dallas?!" I shouted into the phone. "Go to court and fight for yourself by yourself because I'm done! I'd rather be alone for the rest of my miserable life than fuck with you ever again!"

That was it, I hung up on him and dialed my carrier. I had to change my number once again. I had changed my number so many times they no longer waived the $25 fee. But I had to do what I had to do. That was the only way I would ever have any peace...

Chapter Three

Dallas

It took me a whole week to get in contact with Tangi only for her to cuss me out and change her number again. I didn't know where she lived either. Now I was stuck fighting for my rights all alone. My case looked hopeless, but I wasn't gonna stop trying.

Now that the secret affair was out in the open, nothing was hanging over my head except for that "rape" video. That was the one thing that could get Tierra the full custody she was seeking. I had to do something to make sure that shit got deleted and never got out. If Tierra ever found out about that shit, I was doomed.

Sitting at my dining room table taking shots, I plotted on how to get Tangi on my good side or in a position where she needed me. Only I couldn't come up with shit! Now I was getting desperate again and when I got that way, it was all bad.

Picking up my cell again, I dialed Tierra. I knew she was mad at me, but the facts still remained the same. We had a daughter together and whether she liked it or not, I was going to be a part of Miracle's life.

"What the hell are you calling me for, you sorry sack of shit?!" Tierra growled. "You should be ashamed to call yourself Miracle's sperm donor because you don't deserve the 'father' or 'daddy' title, you fuckin' worthless bum!"

"Wow!" I gasped at her harsh words. Tierra had a lot of nerve saying that shit to me. At one time, she'd never speak to me so disrespectfully. But I'd be willing to bet that she'd never say that shit to my face. Shit, I'd waste no time hemming her ass the hell up!

"Wow is right! Wow you're calling me!"

"I'm only trying to do what's best for our daughter. She deserves to have both of her parents in her life. I'm just trying to be reasonable and work something out, so we don't end up going to court behind this shit..."

"You should've thought about that shit when you were fuckin' Tangi, you disgusting bastard!" she insulted.

"Tierra I ain't tryna hear all that shit! I just wanna see my baby girl! I ain't tryna take her away from you or interrupt the happy lil home you and that funny looking nigga over there tryna create..."

"You stupid muthafucka!" Tierra spat angrily. "Don't call my fuckin' phone. I'm gonna abide by the court order and not change my number, but they can't make me answer this muthafucka!"

Tierra hung up on me and ignored my next two calls. That was enough to let me know she was on that bullshit. I knew that she was angry about finding out about me and Tangi, but damn! She was talking to me like I was some random nigga who had wronged her instead of her ex-husband who she shared a child with. She and I had some good times back in the day. I just wanted her to remember those times so we could find a civil way to co-parent Miracle. I wasn't going to let her push me out of our daughter's life so that hulky ass nigga could pretend to be her daddy. No way that shit was about to happen!

Firing up a blunt, I inhaled deeply and began scheming once again. That sativa will have you coming up with shit you would never think of if you weren't high.

This muthafucka Smooth probably at the club right now. I should just go down there and ask the nigga about Tangi. I need to find out where she lives so I can get her to help me out.

What harm could it do? She said the fool was done fucking with her. He must not want her, so why wouldn't he give me the information if he wasn't trying to fuck with her no more?

Pumping myself up to do some more dumb shit, I got showered and dressed then took my ass right on down to their little establishment. I wasn't going to start shit, I just wanted Tangi back.

I'm gonna get her back too!

Confidence filled my body as I blew another blunt on my ride down to the club. It was just what I needed to put me in an untouchable mode.

Keeping the momentum flowing steadily as I walked inside, I boldly strolled to the bar and ordered a drink. Once I had my double shot of Hennessey on the rocks, I found a corner table and watched the back office doors until Smooth appeared. It was damn near closing time by then and I was on full in the liquor department.

Spotting the extra security guards inside, I decided to dip outside undetected and approach Smooth when he came out. I wasn't dumb enough to step to him with his boy nearby, especially with me being as intoxicated as I was.

Shaking the cloudiness from my head, I slipped out the front door then went and got in my car to move it closer to Smooth's ride. I recognized it right off.

Damn, where the hell that nigga at?

Sitting in the car for the next hour, I sobered up a bit as I watched the club empty out. The last two people to exit were Smooth and some light skinned chick. I leaned back in my seat as they exchanged a few friendly words and went their separate ways.

As Smooth neared his ride, I opened my door and got out. His head rose and we locked eyes angrily.

"Nigga I know you ain't coming up here with no bullshit." Smooth chanted with a mean mug.

"Look man, I ain't coming up here to start shit with you. At least not the way you showed up at my job. I'm just worried about Tangi. I heard what happened between her and Tierra and now she's shutting everyone out..."

"When she's ready to talk to you, if she ever is, I'm sure she'll reach out to you. Other than that, I got nothing for you, playa." Smooth clowned with a laugh as he popped his locks.

As he opened the driver's door, I put my hand on it to stop him. "Why the fuck you trippin' if you don't want her?"

"Who the fuck said I didn't want her?" he asked while side eyeing me as he lowered his large buffed frame into his car. "Matter of fact, how the fuck you know we ain't together?"

That nigga had to be fucking with me. Tangi had already told me the whole story. I guess he called himself trying to fuck with my head.

"I know because she told me you wasn't fuckin' with her no more. Now Tierra ain't fuckin' with her, so I'm sure she's probably hurting pretty bad. She needs me."

"Nigga she don't need you! It's your fuckin' fault that she's feeling the fucked up way she does now!" Smooth snapped rising up out of his seat and backing me up.

"Y'all aight out here boss?" one of the three guys approaching asked with his hand on his heater that was partially stuck in his waistband.

"I'm cool. This clown right here was just leaving." Smooth smirked and threw his hands in the air. "We gotta problem?"

"Nah fool!" I huffed and turned to leave. "I'll just find her myself. She needs a man to look out for her since yo joker ass sho' couldn't stand the heat. Tangi made a couple of bad mistakes and you run out on her. Yeah, she don't need a nigga like you."

"Oh, and she need a nigga like you, right?" Jay added as he joined the group. Easing his body in front of everyone, he gazed down at me with hate filled eyes.

"Look, like I told that nigga over there... I didn't come for no trouble I'm just worried about your sister." I said standing my ground while hoping that nigga didn't steal on me. My pistol was in my glove box, but I knew that I couldn't make it there without raising some suspicion.

"She's fine, so you ain't gotta worry about her. Trust me, I got my lil sister taken care of. Now, what you need to do is leave these premises and don't bring yo ass back here!" Jay demanded as he checked the lot.

Watching in the direction of the back entrance where his vision was fixated on, I saw a set of headlights. Jay really got angry then. He walked up on me and threatened to fuck me up if I didn't leave.

"I'll leave. Just let me holler at Tangi right quick. What harm will it do? Shit, she got all you muthafuckas ready to jump a nigga out here! What the fuck am I gonna do? I just wanna make sure she's straight," I pressed as Tangi parked and got out of the car. She walked right by him and punched me in the face. As I lunged back on pure reflex, I was greeted by a series of blows and kicks. I didn't even know who was hitting and who was stomping me. The only thing that I remembered was waking up smelling like piss with a sore and aching body.

Fuck this shit! That's the last ass whoopin' I'm gonna take! Next time I'm gonna load a muthafucka with some hot ones! That's on everything!

Chapter Four

Smooth

That nigga Dallas wasn't gonna learn his lesson. He just kept popping his ass up at the club like it was gonna be something nice when he saw me, or even Jay for that matter.

"Do you believe that clown?" Jay whispered as he motioned for his sister to get in the car. "That nigga ain't gonna stop until I dead his ass!"

"Yeah, that muthafucka is persistent as fuck." I added not taking my eyes off Tangi who was now back in her ride. "What's up with your sister though? How is she?"

"She's gonna be good. I got her. Don't even trip," Jay assured, cutting me off with a huff.

Sure, we just had each other's back behind that fool Dallas, but it was something totally different when it came to Tangi. Jay was still salty about things not working out between me and his sister.

It wasn't that I didn't love her or want to be with her. It was just that so much bad shit had transpired that I didn't know how to start back over with her. I mean, honestly... how could I love her when she didn't love herself? The best thing for me to do was to give Tangi space.

"Well, I'm about to head home. That long ass ride." I complained as I stepped to my car again. "What you about to do bruh?"

"I gotta take Tangi somewhere right quick. She wanna wait until the middle of the night to bug me about some shit," Jay said without looking at me. I knew right then he was lying.

Instead of calling him on it, I drove off with the intentions of dropping by Tangi's before I went home. To kill some time, I went to the Waffle House and got something to eat.

When I finished, I got my cell out to call Tangi, but quickly found out that her number had been changed. I didn't know that she had changed it because I hadn't tried to reach her since she hung up on me that day she and Tierra had it out. I was trying to give her the space that she needed following the blowup. She was trying to put all that shit on me, but it wasn't my fault. I didn't make her betray her best friend. I never forced her to jump in bed with that no good muthafucka. She did all that shit on her own knowing that when Tierra found out, their friendship would be ruined.

Tangi should've never done that shit. That was some foul shit I would've never expected from her. When I met her, she seemed to be so well put together. She seemed like a good woman who had it going on. The whole time, she had been sleeping with her best friend's husband. I should've been done with her ass once I found out about what she had done, but my heart wouldn't let me leave her alone. I loved Tangi, and no matter how bad I wanted to move the hell on, I couldn't shake her.

After what just happened with Dallas, I didn't know how that nigga was gonna react once he woke up in that fucked up condition. I didn't know if he would try to retaliate or what, but I wasn't gonna wait around and find out after the shit happened. That's just why I needed to make sure Tangi was okay.

I parked shamelessly in front of her house wondering where the hell she was, I found myself waiting for more than two hours for her to return. By that time, I had fallen asleep and would've still been knocked out too if Tangi wouldn't have come banging on my window.

Jumping up, I frantically turned to the left to see her standing there looking at me angrily. With no hesitation, I exited my truck and stepped around only to be harshly greeted by her unwelcoming gaze.

"What are you doing here Smooth?" she asked as she crossed her arms over her chest.

"I was worried about you, so I came by to check on you."

"Well, as you can see, I'm just fine. You didn't need to waste your time."

Damn! Why the hell did she still have an attitude with me? I would've thought that would've blown over by now.

"It wasn't a waste of time. Tangi, why you so mad at me though? What did I do?" I asked.

"What did you do? You do realize that my whole friendship with Tierra is over because of you, right?"

"How is that? I wasn't even there when y'all got into it. I never told her what you did..."

"Shit, you may as well have! You kept pushing and pushing me to confess when you knew what would happen if I did that! Why couldn't you have just minded your own damn business?!" I could tell that she was very much hurt by what happened.

"I just wanted you to do the right thing..."

"And doing the 'right thing' as you call it ruined my friendship with my best friend in the whole world!" Tears began to drain from her eyes. All I wanted to do was take her in my arms and take her pain away. If I could carry that pain for her, I'd do it.

I made a move to embrace her, but she pushed me away. "Let me hold you Tangi. Let me be there for you!"

"This is all your fault! I don't want you to be there for me!" she cried.

"Tangi, I love you ma. Don't you see that? I love you so much and all I wanna do is be there for you. If I could take that pain that you're feeling in your heart away, I'd do it in an instant. I know that you're probably questioning every decision you've made in your life, but trust me, this shit between you and me... it wasn't a mistake. I still wanna marry you because of how much I love you. And deep down in your heart, I know that you love me too," I said.

I tried to hug her again and she slapped me across the face.

WHAP!

"What the hell was that for?" I asked.

"That's the slap that Tierra gave me because of you! She slapped me again, so you owe me one more!"

She made a move to slap me again, but that time I grabbed her hand before it made contact with my cheek.

"If it makes you feel better to blame someone else for what you did, fine! But you and I both know that you made a conscious decision to fuck your best friend's husband. You did that, not me or anybody else who you're trying to place the blame on. You did that shit by yourself! I just poured my heart out to you, and instead of cutting me some slack, you swung on me, so you know what? I'm done! I refuse to allow you to use me for a punching bag because you don't wanna put the blame where it belongs... ON YOUR DAMN SELF!!" I was done. I had enough with her bullshit. She needed to hear the truth.

"Whatever! I don't have time for this shit!"

"Good! Oh, by the way, maybe you should call Dallas to come over and stroke your ego for you. You don't want someone that'll give it to you real and straight, so go call the nigga you was bumpin' and grindin' with in the first damn place!" I said as I got back in my truck.

"FUCK YOU SMOOTH!!" she yelled.

Wow! Fuck me, huh? That's what she had for me after everything I had said to her about how I felt... fuck me?! I guess she really didn't give a shit about me. At least not how I cared for her. Instead of responding to her fucked up words that she was throwing at me nonstop, I put my truck in reverse and backed out of her driveway. Tangi would realize soon enough that she put her own self in this position. Not Tierra, not me or anyone else she felt the need to blame.

Until then, I was done...

Chapter Five

Tangi

When I left with my brother, I expected him to drop me off at the airport so that I could go to Oregon, but that didn't happen. I didn't even want to go after that shit with Dallas up at the club. My nerves were wrecked, and I just needed to go lay down in my own bed.

Then, when I finally dropped my brother off and got home, I unexpectedly found Smooth sitting there waiting for me when I pulled up in my driveway. My heart skipped a beat because I was happy to see him. But then I remembered that it was because of him that Tierra had found out about me and Dallas. If he had left well enough alone, she still wouldn't know anything. Thanks to him and his bullshit phone call, she now knew everything. So, yes, I had an attitude with him. I didn't even know what he was doing here and I just spazzed out without thinking.

After I slapped him that first time, it felt good, but I owed him two. That second one didn't happen though because he stopped me, cussed me out and left! *Ugh!* Once he drove off, I went inside still feeling pissed at him for what he said.

With a major attitude, I made my way to the bathroom to take a shower. As I passed the mirror, I caught a glimpse of my reflection. I hadn't been able to look myself in the eye since Tierra found out what Dallas and I had done. But now I was standing there taking a long hard look at myself and I didn't like what I saw at all. I couldn't believe the person I had become. I couldn't believe that I had done such an awful thing to ruin my best friend's marriage. Smooth was right. That shit was all my fault.

I hated the person staring back at me. Tierra had been there for me through every heartache and breakup that I had experienced. She always had positive words for me and a shoulder to lean on. She dried my tears more than I had dried hers. She was more like a big sister to me instead of a best friend and I had ruined it all with my selfishness.

I was the worse friend she could've possibly had. Honestly, I had fucked up, not Smooth. The person staring at me should be ashamed of herself, and I was. Before I could stop myself, I grabbed the ceramic toothbrush holder on the counter and slammed it into the mirror, splitting the image of myself into broken shards of glass.

"DON'T LOOK AT ME!!" I yelled as I smashed it again. My hand was bleeding, but I didn't care.

How could I look at myself and not feel disgrace? I was a disgusting human being. My best friend had just had a baby and I should be there for her, but I couldn't because I had fucked up.

My bags are still packed and in the car! Maybe I should just leave! Maybe I should just run away! No one will miss me but my brother and that's the only person who will know where I am!

Crying loudly, I showered, and bandaged my cut hand then I turned on my computer and got online to change my flight. Luckily, I was able to book one for that morning at 6am and I made it in time to park in the extended lot. The guy there guided me to the shuttle landing, and I was able to ride one over to the terminal.

The next step was getting through the security gate. Damn, it was a fucking hassle just to board!

I didn't even realize how terrified I was of flying until I got on that plane, buckled up and it took off. It was like a ride at the amusement park. The one that snatched your whole body backward and pinned you to your seat. I was hanging on like a hub cap in the fast lane.

"I need a drink!" I yelled out to the stewardess that quickly came to me to let me know that it would be a while before she could bring the drink cart out.

"Fuck that rude bitch!" The older white woman shrugged as she dug in her backpack and came out with a plastic gallon sized Ziplock baggie filled with shot bottles. "You want vodka or tequila love?"

"Are you supposed to bring that on here?!" I whispered forcibly lowering her hand. She cracked up so loudly that her face turned red.

"Yeah, you can bring them on. They really don't want you to drink them on board because they claim they can't monitor your alcohol intake, but the hell with them! Let's drink!"

"Okay, well I'll take one of those Patron shots!"

"Take three!" she chuckled heartily and shoved them into my lap.

Opening the first one, I downed it, and washed it down with the six-dollar bottle of water that I bought inside the airport. I followed it up with a second and then the third. Now I was nice and relaxed. I even dozed off.

"Hey, we're in Portland!" the lady sang out with the strong scent of tequila spewing from mouth. That was enough to bounce me out of my seat and grab my bag in the overhead compartment.

Scurrying by her, I exited the plane and went to get my luggage before I pulled up my app to get an Uber. I didn't need a rental since Jay had a Dodge Journey out at his house.

"Ugh!" I grunted as I went out front to meet the driver. My stomach turned forcing the contents upward. Leaning to the side and tilting my head, I was able to release it all in the trash receptacle.

Hastening to get my bottled water out, I rinsed my mouth out a couple of times then got some gum out my purse. Now my head was spinning.

"Oh shit!" I yelled out as the red minivan began to pull up. Jogging with my hands full, I caught him at the pedestrian crossing.

"Sorry about that ma'am." The young handsome driver apologized as he jumped out with his long dreads bouncing as he helped put my bags in the back.

"It's okay. I wasn't paying attention and didn't see that the alert went off telling me you were here." I admitted as I got in and checked my cell for the time and also the driver's name because I had forgotten it that fast. "Damn, that was 15 minutes ago. I'm sorry McAdoo."

"It's okay Tangi. Sometimes the reception out here ain't too good." He replied using my first name as we swerved through the traffic to get on the highway. "This your first time in Portland?"

"Yes. Does it always rain like this?" I sulked as the heavy rain pounded on the windows.

Not allowing the weather to dampen my expectations of my trip, I tried focusing on the beautiful green landscaping that we passed along the highway. There were rows and rows of trees and plenty of mountains in the distance.

"Which one is Mount Hood?" I questioned anxiously as my tummy began to grumble.

"That one right there!" the driver pointed.

"That looks far!" I said feeling hungry.

"Yeah, the drive out there is about an hour and fifteen minutes..."

"Oh, no! I can't wait that long! I'm starving! Can we please stop by a drive thru or something?! I'm sure my brother doesn't have food at his place and that means I'm gonna have to go to the grocery store... nah! I gotta eat."

"Okay, okay!" McAdoo laughed as I pulled up My Maps and located food spots along I-205 heading south.

The driver was more than happy to take me to Elmer's Restaurant that I found on my app. It was right off the freeway. Calling ahead of time, I preordered some food for both of us. So much for doing that shit... when we got there, our orders still weren't ready!

As we waited, I pulled out my cell and saw my empty incoming call log. Making a hasty decision, I opened up my contacts and deleted all of them except for Jay's.

That way I couldn't reach anyone because I no longer had their info, and no one could reach me because I had a new number! It was all good!

"Order for a Tangi!" The lady behind the register announced, sending my mind right back to food. We both went up to get it.

"McAdoo, I don't really want to eat here. You mind if we get it to go?" I asked not feeling comfortable enough to sit face to face with a stranger while grubbing.

"Nah, I'm cool with that and I appreciate the meal," he laughed.

Back on the road, I listened to McAdoo smack loudly as he told me all about this private taxi company he started up. His idea pinged off Uber, but had more perks and personal touches.

"I started out working in customer service in Portland. From there I went to the Greenlight Hub then a driver. I learned as much as I could and with the help of my girl, we're making this shit happen!" he boasted in between bites. "I'm gonna keep working for these muthafuckas until my business gets off the ground."

It was so good seeing young black men doing positive things. The streets were heartless and nothing but trouble. The best thing to do was to stay out of them!

"Is it snowing?" I asked losing my train of thought as the snowflakes fell lightly.

"Yeah, a few inches are supposed to fall tonight." He stated as we turned down an unpaved narrow road until we came upon a Victorian style home. It was way bigger than it looked in the pamphlet Jay had printed up.

"This shit looks like a damn plantation! What the hell did my brother go and buy?"

"Nah, this shit is nice!" McAdoo yelled out. "This is that Airbnb that my homeboy rented last month! This is your brother's place?!"

McAdoo pulled as close as he could to the stairs leading to the wrap around porch. I was still in disbelief until I used the key to open the front door then followed the instructions to disarm the alarm.

"See, I told you this shit is nice!" McAdoo said excitedly from behind me before setting my bags in the foyer.

Tipping him generously, I showed his ass right back to the door and thanked him. After closing and locking the door behind him, I reset the alarm then went to find the bathroom. I had been holding my pee for the last half hour.

Ring, ring, ring...

Right off, I knew it was my brother. It totally slipped my mind about calling him after I decided to go to Oregon after all.

Damn! I forgot to call Jay!

Flying back to the foyer where I dropped my purse, I got my cell out and answered it. "I'm sorry…"

"What the hell you leave like that for?!" he shouted angrily. "I went by your house and been fuckin' callin' your phone Tangi!"

"Well how did you know where I was?"

"Because you disarmed the alarm at the spot! That shit don't matter though sis! I've been fuckin' flippin' the hell out not knowing where you were! You even made me hem that nigga Smooth up!"

Oh shit! Perhaps I should've contacted him sooner…

Chapter Six

Smooth

"Nigga, I told you I ain't seen her since around 2 this morning!" I snapped when I walked into the club that night and Jay pulled me aside with a nasty fucking attitude. "I ain't got no reason to lie to you bruh!"

"Well that's how long her ass been missin'!" Jay barked as he came in my face and tried to back me into the bar. "Let me call her ass one more time."

Trying to peek down at his cell to memorize Tangi's number, all I could see was her name and a picture of her beautiful face. That shit was useless.

"Tangi!" Jay yelled into his phone as he turned away and left me standing there. That nigga seriously thought I had done something to Tangi! I loved that girl and there he was trying to fight me behind some dumb assumption. Like what fucking reason would I have to do something to her? I was trying to get her to clear her conscious so I could marry her. Like damn! I was so mad that I was ready to go cuss his ass out and check him for even thinking that I would do anything to hurt his sister.

"Let me wait 'til that fool get off the phone." I mumbled as I yelled for the bartender to pour me a double.

As I lifted the glass to my mouth, Jay was coming back out to apologize. "My bad, man. It's just that all this shit with my sister got me stressed the fuck out! First, she loses the baby, then y'all break up, now her and Tierra done fell out behind that sorry ass nigga Dallas! I swear I'm gonna end up fuckin' that fool up if he don't leave Tangi the hell alone!"

Jay nodded his head to signal the bartender for his drink and was served before I could try to put in my bid for another one. "I understand that's your sister and all, but bruh... I wouldn't do shit to hurt that girl. Even though we ain't together, I still got mad love for her. She's the one that shooed me off this time. I tried to work it out with her when I went over there and waited for hours for her to come home..."

"Damn, nigga you sound a lil whipped." Jay clowned as he held his fist out.

Pounding mine against his, I smiled and asked about Tangi. "So, how is she doing? She cool?"

"I'on even know! The crazy girl just got up and left on the damn plane..."

Suddenly Jay caught himself and stopped talking. His expressions showed that he had slipped up and told me some shit he shouldn't have.

"She left town?!" I asked while my heart dropped. "For good?"

"I ain't said shit and don't hold me to sayin' no shit. She'll get in touch with you if she wants to talk..."

"Just shoot me her number so I can check on her..."

"Nah, she'd kill me if I did some shit like that nigga! Stop playin'!" Jay laughed as he set his empty glass on the bar and put his cell in his pocket.

"Nah, it's cool. Just tell her that I was asking about her and if she wants to talk..."

"Yeah, I'll relay that message, but you don't know how stubborn my sister can be. She may not be gone for good, but no telling when her ass is coming back."

"What? Y'all got family somewhere?"

"See, now yo ass is prying Smooth!" Jay laughed as he lifted his set of keys out of his front pocket. "I'll tell her that you were askin' about her though bruh."

That night at work, it was busier than usual. I couldn't get shit done with Tangi on my mind and these half-dressed stank butt bitches in my grill every five fucking minutes. I wasn't thinking about none of them and clearly made it known that I gave zero fucks about how rude I was being.

Checking my phone for the time, I saw that it was later than I thought. It was thirty minutes to closing time.

Feeling tired and hungry, I had the head of security for the club close and lock up for me since there was nothing but two or three patrons still in there. It was so dead and boring that I couldn't stay another fucking second.

Sneaking out the back door to escape this one clingy broad named Syirra that was a regular, I rushed to my car only to find that nigga Dallas leaned up against it. Before I could get to him, he lifted up his shirt and displayed a handgun.

"Nigga I promise that you will never catch me slippin' again!" he slurred as he struggled to stand up properly. His slouch, disheveled appearance and his jumbled speech told me that he was fucking drunk and maybe even high. "You came into our lives and fucked everything up! Tangi and I were happy before you started fucking with her. I left my wife to be with her! Then you and yo boys gonna jump me and piss on me?!"

Drawing down, Dallas aimed his gun at my face. His trembling hands clinched the trigger making me tense up.

"What? You ain't got yo heater tonight nigga?" Dallas laughed as he walked closer. "Don't tell me I caught you slippin'?!"

Now this nigga just had to get bold one of the few times I left home without my nine. I hadn't been carrying it lately because I had a bad temper and didn't want to do no stupid shit. That definitely would've been the night!

Look at me now! Out here without no heat! Where the fuck was Jay or security?!

As I glanced up at the cameras monitoring the lot, I saw that the red light wasn't blinking. That meant it wasn't even working.

"Don't look for help now nigga! All you gotta do is tell me where Tangi is or give me her fuckin' number!" Spit flew out his mouth as he threatened me with the chrome revolver.

Just as I lunged to try to take the gun from Dallas' drunk ass, out of nowhere Jay came flying out of the darkness and tackled him. That nigga Dallas hopped up like a crackhead and held the gun on both of us.

"Jay, nigga where's your fuckin' heat?" I whispered wondering why Jay jumped on Dallas and didn't get the fucking gun?!

"Especially when yo ass ain't packin'! Nigga!" Dallas yelled ending my rant. "Tell me where Tangi is!"

Sirens rang in the distance bringing all of our attention to the end of the block where the red and blue lights were reflecting off the nearby glass building. "Right on time!" I smiled and turned around only to hear tires screeching. Just like that... the nigga was in the wind.

"See! That's why I'm gonna have to fuck that nigga up bruh!" Jay snapped and pulled his pistol out the back of his waistband.

"What?!" I yelled and bent down to catch my breath from all the anxiety. "You had a gun and didn't shoot that nigga! He could've killed us!"

"Nah, he ain't gonna do shit but live his last days in misery. Next time I catch him, it's lights out for that nigga! On my fam Smooth! He done went too far this time!"

Using the situation to my advantage, I asked about Tangi again and urged him to call and check on her again in front of me. "That nigga is on a rampage. Just make sure she's cool bruh."

Jay fell for that shit and dialed Tangi up. He didn't put her on speaker, but I could hear her faintly. "Jay, I thought you were gonna call when you got off?"

"I'm off now. I'm about to go to the house. I just wanted to check on you. I just looked at the forecast...

it's cold there huh?" Jay paused and paced a little closer to me. "That house is the truth tho' huh sis?!"

Listening closely, I slowly began to gather information to help me find out where Tangi was hiding out. I know I told her that I was done with her, but I wasn't. I couldn't be! I was just a sucka in love! Jay knew it too when he caught me staring down his throat.

"So, what about that view sis?" Jay asked Tangi then suddenly looked over at me noticing that I was ear hustling. He cut that whole conversation short.

Again, that nigga knew he was talking too much, and I was taking it all in. I wasn't missing a beat!

Yeah, they didn't call me Smooth for nothing....

Chapter Seven

Tierra

One week later...

Things had been going so good! Thaddeus and I were great! Miracle was getting bigger and more beautiful every day and I couldn't have felt more blessed.

Peace had been with me for the past few days because I hadn't heard from Dallas or Tangi and I was totally fine with that. It gave me the chance to focus on my family.

All that went to shit when Dallas came by my house with that fucking gun after midnight that Saturday. I went to the door thinking that Thaddeus had gotten locked out and found that crazy asshole of an ex-husband on my doorstep! He was looking retarded and smelling like an alcohol brewery.

"Ew! What the hell do you want Dallas?" I asked.

He showed the gun, but I wasn't going to show him that I was scared...even though every bone in my body was shaking. I had a daughter to protect, so now was not the time for me to show weakness.

"I wanna see my daughter," he said.

"Hell no!"

"Tierra I'm not asking you. I'm telling you that I want to see my daughter!" That time, he raised the gun and pointed it at me.

"You don't scare me Dallas!" I said as I gulped hard. I only hoped and prayed that my voice didn't give away how I truly felt inside. I was also hoping that Thaddeus would hurry up and get here. "You think that I'm going to let you anywhere near my baby at this time of night when you're drunk and smelling like a wino? You better get off my damn property before I call the police on your ass!"

"I wanna see my daughter Tierra! You can't keep her from me! I'm her father!"

"Get away from here Dallas! You think I'm playing when I say I'm gonna call the police?" I threatened.

"I'll have your head blown off before you can grab your phone!" he threatened back.

"I already have my phone." I lied hoping that he fell for that shit and moved along. "All I have to do is dial 911. Now, are you ready to go to jail tonight? Because you know that you will for two reasons...one, for showing up here and threatening me with a gun and two, for driving while drunk! Go home!"

He scratched his head as he seemed to be thinking about what I said. Then he put the gun away and looked at me. "I'ma go, but know that I'm coming back to see my little girl. You can't keep her from me. I deserve to see her," he said in a slurred tone.

I didn't give two shits about what he said or how he felt. All I wanted him to do was get the hell away from my doorstep. As he staggered to his car, I watched him struggle to open the door. Once he had done that, he slid into the seat and started the car. I prayed that he made it home safe and didn't crash into anybody while on the road.

Shutting the door quickly, I leaned against it as I breathed a sigh of relief. I couldn't believe how calm I was even when my life was being threatened.

Inhaling then exhaling one last time, I spun around, locked the door and went to check on my baby girl. Upon entering her room, I found her still sound asleep, oblivious to the threat her mommy just faced at the hands of her father. If Dallas had just taught me anything, it was that I needed to protect my daughter with everything in me. I was going to apply for a protective order as soon as the courthouse opened tomorrow. I was going to show the surveillance video from my home security cameras and once the judge saw Dallas waving the gun at me, I knew I'd get that order of protection barring him from my property.

Damn dummy is burying himself deeper everyday...

Thankfully, I didn't have to be home and worry alone for long. Thaddeus came in 10 minutes later and I rushed into his arms. My body trembled and shook as he held me even though I always felt safe in them before.

"What's going on? You alright?" he asked, concern evident in his voice.

I shook my head no and held onto him for dear life. "Dallas was just here..."

"What?" he asked. "Did he hurt you?"

He pulled back and looked me up and down.

"No, but he had a gun!" I cried.

"He had a what?!"

"He had a gun! I was so scared babe! I really think he's gone off the deep end and he's gonna hurt me to get to Miracle!"

"I don't want you to think about that! He ain't gonna do shit to hurt you or Miracle... I can promise you that!"

"How can you be so sure? He could've shot me tonight!" I said. "I'm going get a TRO first thing tomorrow."

"That nigga is a coward! If he was gonna shoot you, trust me, he would've done so already!" Thaddeus reasoned. "To be sure though, tomorrow, we're gonna go to the courthouse and get a TRO against his ass. That nigga is definitely getting bolder with his shit. From now on, I don't want you opening the door without checking the cameras first. Got it?"

I nodded my head affirmatively as he took me in his arms again. I started crying because I really was scared of Dallas tonight. I wasn't taking any chances with his ass no more. I couldn't believe he had taken it there. I mean, out of all the shit he had done to me, I would've never tried to hurt him like he did me. He had nerve to be upset that I was keeping Miracle from him, but what he did tonight didn't change my mind one bit. If anything, it made me see how right I was to keep my daughter from his ass.

The next morning, I got up early and while my mom watched the baby, Thaddeus and I went down to the courthouse. I had to get this restraining order to protect my family. I was going to make sure that Dallas never got to see our little girl until he got a mental evaluation and took some anger management courses. He was obviously becoming unglued and was very dangerous.

Just as I got into a serious mental rant, we were arriving at the courthouse. It was early and they were just opening up the doors.

With the security footage from this morning in hand, I requested a restraining order for both me and my little girl, Miracle. When the judge took one look at the evidence, it was all over for Dallas.

The papers were drawn up and I was walking out of the courthouse an hour later with a restraining order in hand. Because he had threatened me with a gun, Dallas couldn't come within 100 feet of me or my daughter or he'd be in violation.

On top of that shit, a warrant had been issued for his arrest because he came onto my property and threatened my life. I would've loved to be a fly on the wall when they served him with the papers and slapped the cuffs on him. He deserved to rot in jail for scaring the shit out of me the way that he did.

I hope they lock him up and throw the damn key away...

Chapter Eight

Dallas

If someone had told me that I'd regret the path that I had taken, I wouldn't have believed them. After all, things had been working in my favor... well, except for Tierra not letting me see my daughter, Tangi's disappearing act, and almost getting jumped by those two lunatics. Well, I guess shit hadn't been going my way at all. But after I showed up at Tierra's house, I just knew that she'd be calling me soon to see my daughter, at least I hoped so.

BANG! BANG! BANG!

The banging of the door awakened me out of my drunken sleep. I didn't know what time it was or who was at the door, but I got up from the sofa and slowly made my way to answer it. You could imagine the look on my face when I opened the door and two police officers stood there with papers in hand.

"Mr. Dallas Armstrong?" one of them inquired.

"Who wants to know?" I asked.

"Are you Mr. Armstrong?"

"Look man, I had a long night and I'm not in the mood for this shit!" I said as I tried to close the door.

"Sir, I'm going to have to ask you to step outside please," the cop ordered.

I did as I was told since I was outnumbered two to one. "What the hell is this about?"

"I have a warrant for your arrest..."

"A WARRANT?! WHAT THE HELL FOR?!" I asked.

"For threatening your ex-wife with a firearm." As the cuffs were slapped on my wrists, the other cop began reading my Miranda rights.

What the hell is really going on? Did Tierra really call the cops on me? That answer slapped me across the face like a ton of bricks as I was shoved into the back seat of the cruiser.

As the cops climbed into the front seat, I was told about the charges and restraining order Tierra had filed this morning. *Why would she do this shit to me? I'm the father of her child!*

When we got down to the station, I was hustled inside. They fingerprinted me and booked me, then stuck me in a holding cell. I got to make my one phone call and didn't know who the hell to call.

After silently debating for a bit, I decided to call my mom since she didn't know what was going on between me and Tierra. I knew she would come.

By the time I was bailed out, five hours later, I felt like a prisoner. I collected my belongings, which included the protective order, and headed outside to meet my mom.

"Thanks for coming mom," I said as I hugged her.

She immediately pushed me away. "What the hell is going on with you Dallas? Why were you arrested? And why do you smell like yesterday's trash?" She lifted her nose in the air as if I stunk really bad.

"Mom, it's a long story. Can we just go? This place is making me itch..."

"It ain't the place that's making you itch son. You smell like shit! You ass is itching because it needs to be washed in disinfectant!" she complained as we headed to her car. "Oh God! I'm gonna have to get my whole car fumigated!"

I turned to look at her with a smirk on my face. "Really mom? Fumigated?"

"Boy, do you smell yourself?! Oh God! We are going to have to ride with the windows down and you know how I feel about my damn wigs!" she said. She took her wig off and threw it on the back seat so it wouldn't get messed up in the wind. Now she was over there looking like Queen Latifah in 'Set it off'.

"Sorry mom."

"What's going on?" She asked as she backed out of the parking space and stabbed her big bodied Benz onto the street. "Why were you arrested?"

"Tierra pressed charges on me."

"TIERRA PRESSED CHARGES ON YOU?! FOR WHAT?!" she asked.

"It's a long story..."

"Then tell it because I have time."

"Mom, I really don't feel like talking about this."

"I don't give two shits whether you feel like discussing it or not! I just bailed your ass out of jail, so you are going to explain to me why I had to do that! Now talk!"

I knew when my mom used that tone I had no choice but to respond. I hadn't told her much about me and Tierra's relationship... she didn't even know that I had left her or anything. She did know about Tierra being pregnant, but didn't know she had Miracle yet because of everything that had been going on. So, I gave her the rundown as she drove me home.

"So, you mean to tell me that Tierra had the baby and I never got sent a picture or anything?" she fumed.

"I'm sorry. I've been trying to get her to let me see my own daughter, but that's like pulling teeth."

"Why won't she let you see your own baby?"

"I don't know. I guess cuz she's moved on, she'd rather pretend that the other nigga is the daddy," I said.

"No, no, no! That's not how this is gonna work! That's your baby and you deserve to see your child!"

"I know mom, but she won't let me!"

"That's bullshit! What's her address?"

"We can't just show up over there! Well, I can't anyway!" I said.

"What do you mean?" she asked.

"She has a restraining order against me. I can't come within 100 feet of her or my daughter," I said. That shit broke my heart. I didn't even realize that I was crying until my mom brushed away a tear.

"Don't cry baby. As soon as I drop you off, I'm gonna go over there and find out what the hell is going on! This shit is ridiculous!" my mom fussed. "She can't take her issues with you out on your relationship with your baby! That baby is just as much yours as it is hers!"

"I know but..."

"Ain't no buts about it! You deserve to be in your child's life and I'm gonna make sure that happens!"

She drove me to my house and then told me send her Tierra's address. Even though I didn't want to, I did it. If my mom could help Tierra see that keeping me from our daughter was wrong then I was all for it. She had to see that what she was doing was a mistake.

While my mom went over to talk to Tierra, I jumped in the shower. My mom was right, I did smell like shit. What the hell was happening to my life? What kind of role model would I be for Miracle in the situation I was in? People had fucked over me left and right since I decided to leave Tierra, especially Tangi. She was the main reason I walked away from my pregnant wife and where the hell was she? Nowhere to be found.

Tangi had forced me to choose between her and Tierra then when I finally did it, she moved on with macho man. What kind of shit was that? Maybe this whole time Tangi had been playing me for a fool. I hoped that wasn't the case because the way I felt these days, that wasn't the right thing to do.

I just knew that something had to give. My mom had to get Tierra to let me see my baby girl because from the looks of things, Miracle was all I had left.

Chapter Nine

Ms. Armstrong

I didn't know who was calling me from jail, so when I heard my son's voice on the other line, I almost shitted on myself. What the hell was my son doing behind bars? I had raised my kids to do the right thing at all times, so Dallas winding up in jail was not something me or my husband would've planned for...God rest Arthur's soul. I really wish my husband was here to help me deal with Dallas and his messes, but since he wasn't, I was going to have to put on my big girl panties and get it done. I just prayed Tierra wouldn't slam the door in my face because then we'd really have problems.

KNOCK! KNOCK! KNOCK!

I waited patiently for her to open the door. As I glanced around the lovely property I smiled. Even though I wish she and my son had stayed together, it wasn't my place to argue with her over it. Dallas walked out on her, so she should've divorced him. He left her while she was pregnant, and I hadn't raised him to be that way.

"Hello Tierra," I greeted when she came to the door shocked to see me. I had no beef with her, so I sure hoped she didn't have any with me. I mean, the two of us had always gotten along. Whatever issues she had with my son had nothing to do with her and I.

"Momma Armstrong, what are you doing here?" she greeted me with a warm hug as she tightly gripped a baby monitor device in her hand.

"May I come in?" I asked.

"Of course," she said as she stepped aside.

So far, so good. Let's hope the rest of our visit goes this smoothly because I hate to bring out the old me and fuck some shit up.

Calming my attitude, I entered into Tierra's beautifully decorated home. I instantly admired her taste. The house she previously shared with my son was nice, but not nearly as elegant as this one. She had definitely moved on up.

See, I raised Dallas on Section 8 and food stamps. It wasn't until I met Howard, a handsome suga daddy, that I began to experience the finer things in life.

Howard Armstrong fell hard for me quickly. Within months, he married me and adopted Dallas, treating him as his own kid. Since then we had worked hard to establish and uphold a prestigious name for ourselves. Now, Tierra was trying to tarnish that. I couldn't let that happen.

Not wanting to be rude, I began with asking about the baby. I was anxious to see my granddaughter and couldn't wait to hear why the hell she was keeping her away from her father; my son! I mean, no matter what issues she and Dallas had going on, it had nothing to do with his ability to be a father to his baby girl. Dallas would never do anything to hurt Miracle and Tierra should know that. If she didn't know, she'd know before I left her house. That baby deserved to have her father in her life and she would if I had anything to do with it.

"I'm sorry for just stopping by like this Tierra, especially without calling first, but Dallas just told me about Miracle. I just had to see her."

"Yes, it was a difficult road but she's here..."

"Can I see her?"

"I just put her down for her nap Momma Armstrong. I would go wake her, but she's been so fussy lately..."

"It's okay. You can at least let me get a peek in on her please. I promise to be quiet and not disturb her."

Tierra had to know that I wasn't going to give up that easily, so she went ahead and gestured me through the long corridor. Passing a set of double doors, we entered the next single one that was partially open.

Pushing it enough for us to pass through, Tierra led me into a nursey that looked professionally decorated. It was like something out of a damn magazine.

"Shhh," Tierra sang as Miracle began to stir around in her crib.

As we neared her, she lifted her head just a bit and opened her eyes. She was looking right at me.

"Aww, she is the most adorable baby I've ever seen!" I gasped with tears in my eyes. "I'm a grandma!"

Miracle began to whimper, and whine and I couldn't resist. I just had to pick her up. "Don't cry honey." I rocked her in my arms as she clung securely to my shirt. She smelled so good! I held her close as I inhaled her sweet scent of baby powder and baby wash.

"Aww, Tierra!" I cried again in disbelief.

Suddenly Miracle began crying loudly. I began to try and soothe her. I swung her, rocked her, sang to her and nestled her, but nothing was working.

"Here, let me see if I can get her quiet." Tierra offered scooping my granddaughter out of my grip.

Same thing! Tierra couldn't get her quiet either. She changed her diaper, tried to feed her, patted her back to release gas and even put her in the swing.

Screaming at the top of her lungs for going on thirty minutes was working my nerves and had me worried. I was almost ready to rush her little butt to the damn emergency room.

"What's wrong baby girl?" A tall fine ass man came into the room and chanted in a child's voice. As he nodded at me with a smile, he went and gently took Miracle from Tierra's arms. "What's she doin' to the baby, huh?"

It was amazing how quickly my granddaughter hushed up as soon as he began to cradle her. She was so quiet as she gazed up at the handsome man holding her. It was hard to believe that she was just screaming a few seconds ago. It was like a totally different baby.

"Oh, so you're just gonna be good for Thaddeus huh?" Tierra giggled as she introduced me to who I assumed was her boyfriend and the real fucking reason that Dallas couldn't see Miracle.

I wanted to let her ass have it right then, but I couldn't act a fool in front of the baby like that. "Nice to meet you Thaddeus."

Eyeing the interaction between this stranger and my granddaughter wasn't sitting well with me at all. The more I thought about how he got to hold her, and my son couldn't even see her had me flaming on the inside.

"I don't mean to be rude, and hate to interrupt your little family time, but exactly why are you keeping Miracle from her father? You know he called me in tears about not being able to see her..."

"Let's go in the living room and talk." Tierra suggested so that we could discuss the matter in private. It didn't matter to me one way or the other because I was sure that this Thaddeus guy knew everything anyway.

Hell, I wouldn't be surprised if he wasn't the one in her ear steering her away from Dallas. Sure, they've had some obstacles between them, but that didn't change the fact that Dallas was still Miracle's father. No matter what Tierra wanted, she couldn't change the DNA running through my granddaughter's veins. She would always have my son's blood pumping inside her.

"Momma Armstrong, before you get the wrong idea..."

"Wrong idea about what? About you shacking up with another man before the ink even dries on your divorce papers, or the wrong idea about having another man playing daddy to my son's daughter?" I snapped with narrowed eyes.

"Whoa!"

"Whoa? Shit, I'm just getting started honey!" I yelled getting a little louder as I walked up on her, daring her ass to jump bad.

You can take the chick out of the hood, but you can't take the hood out of the chick and this Houston hood chick was ready to wreak havoc all up and through this bitch if need be!

"Look Momma Armstrong! Your son and I aren't together because he left me for another woman..."

"I know all about Dallas' dirty deeds, but that still doesn't have anything to do with whether or not he gets to see his baby or not! You are letting your personal feelings for my son keep him from seeing his daughter, and that's not fair!"

"Fair? You wanna talk about fair! Well, how about the woman Dallas was fucking was my best friend Tangi!" she shouted with tears flooding her eyes. "He's the one who asked for a damn divorce! He's the one who walked out on me while I was pregnant to pursue a relationship with my best friend! And he's the one who came over here the other night with a fucking gun threatening to kill me! That's why his ass got locked up! That's why he can't see Miracle and if you ever come over here again acting crazy and disrespectful to me again, you won't be seeing her either! Matter of fact... you can go right now! Get the hell out of my house!" Tierra hollered forcing me toward her, only Thaddeus came running out in time to save her ass. It was this bitch's lucky day cuz I was about to tear that ass up!

"I'll go, but know that me and my son aren't going anywhere! Miracle will be part of our lives whether you like it or not Tierra! You can make this easy or hard... the choice is yours!"

"Well, let me make this choice right now!" Opening the front door widely, Tierra shoved me by the shoulder sending me stumbling down the walkway. I didn't fall, so I was able to spring my big ass up and go after her. Too bad the door was already slammed and locked in my face.

"You better watch yo damn back lil girl! You ain't too grown to get yo ass whooped!" I yelled through the door. "Fuck this shit!"

Straightening my wig on my head, I noticed she had caused me to scuff my expensive shoe. "That lil bitch gon' fuck around and make me choke her ass out. These young bitches today don't know shit about respect. She gon' make me open up an ol' skool can of whoop ass on her. That shit would straighten her mind out real quick.

I huffed heavily as I made my way to my car and got in. I needed to go find my son and have a deep conversation with his ass. It seemed as though he neglected to tell me some important shit that I should've known before coming over here to argue for him. That nigga had a whole lot of explaining to do...

Assuming that my son was at home feeling sorry for himself, I went right on over there to let him have it! That shit Tierra accused him of doing had to be a lie! There was no way that Dallas could have been fucking with Tangi! That girl had been his wife's best friend since they were little kids for Christ's sake. Surely, my son wasn't that disrespectful.

Oooooo, I swear if he did that dirty shit, I'm gonna fuck him up my damn self! He couldn't be that damn dumb!

Half an hour later, I pulled up to my son's place and rang the doorbell. Since he had just moved, he hadn't given me an emergency key to this place yet. It was good that he hadn't kept me waiting long because I was already 380 degrees hot behind the shit Tierra had just told me.

"Dallas, what the hell is going on?! You had me go over to that girl's house without giving me the whole story..."

"What do you mean the whole story? What more did you need to know besides she won't let me see my child?"

"Uh, you know exactly what else I needed to know..."

"Oh, so I guess she told you about me and Tangi!" Dallas sulked with a bottle of whiskey in one hand and a glass of ice in the other.

Glancing around, I noticed that the place was spotless. It didn't even look like he lived here. The only thing that needed cleaning was the sink full of glasses. There wasn't even one dirty plate or bowl.

"What the fuck is wrong with you Dallas? Have you even been eating or just drinking yourself stupid?!"

"I'm in love with Tangi, okay mom! I left Tierra to be with her!"

"Oh wow! I was hoping that Tierra had the story all wrong, but you really did that stupid shit?"

"I fell in love with her mom. It's not my fault the heart wants what it wants! And don't call me stupid!"

"Okay DUMMY! So, where is Tangi now?" I asked him as I stood there with my hands on my hips.

"Huh?" he asked as he stared at me with a stupid expression on his face.

"You left your wife for her best friend, so where is she?"

"Now that right there, is something I wish I knew!" Dallas laughed and cried all at once.

Lord help me! My son is seriously losing it!

Feeling both helpless and sorry for Dallas, I bent down and hugged him tightly. It was something that I hadn't done in years. I was so glad he had washed his ass like I advised, otherwise, I still wouldn't be hugging him.

"It will be okay son..."

"No! No, it won't mom! Not this time. It won't be okay until I find Tangi. I need her!"

My son's pleas pierced my heart. He was wrong as hell for what he had done, but I had to be there for him. Dallas had no one else but me.

"Mom, will you help me? Huh? Will you please help me find Tangi? I love her so much!"

"Yes, I'll help you." I told him and then thought to myself how I was going to ring that heffa's neck as soon as I did find the little homewrecker! She had busted up a perfectly good marriage with her shenanigans.

That bitch got it comin'!

Chapter Ten

Tangi

A few weeks later...

By the way Jay kept calling me at least twice a day for the past three weeks, I knew something was up. I didn't care how cool him and Smooth were, my brother better not have told him where I was. The last thing I needed was him popping up over here and me falling weak.

"Let me call his ass and see what he's up to." I said out loud as I got my phone out and dialed him up.

"What's up sis, you good?" he answered with concern.

"Every time I call you Jay, don't mean that something is wrong. I just miss you."

"Aww, yo ass is homesick, huh?" he teased.

"No, I'm enjoying myself!" I lied. I had come down with some type of virus that only the fresh air could cure. When I was inside, I felt sick and when I went outside, I was good.

Since I hadn't really had an appetite, I had lost about ten pounds. I had even started walking this two-mile trail that wrapped around the property and by the lake. Hood River Oregon was so beautiful!

"Tangi!" Jay shouted jerking me from my thoughts as I gazed out of the picture window from the living room. "Did you hear a word I just said? I done repeated myself at least three times!"

"Huh?"

"What are you doing staring out the window?" my brother laughed. "Come outside and help me with this stuff!"

Throwing the phone down in excitement, I flew to the door and ran out to jump into Jay's arms. It felt so good to have some company!

"Damn! You are homesick!" he teased drawing back from me. "Yo ass done lost some more weight?! Over here looking like America's Next Top Model!"

"Hush Jay!" I giggled as I helped him carry his bags inside. "I have been walking everyday around the trail though."

"It looks good on you sis! You look happy and healthy." He complimented as he got on his phone and frowned.

"What's wrong?"

"My fuckin' cell is dead and I gotta make this call to the club. I was supposed to take care of some shit and I left my boy to do it. I gotta make sure that shit is done."

"Plug it up and use mine," I offered handing it to him. "Let me go clean myself up."

Skipping off to the bedroom filled with happiness, I rushed through the shower and got dressed. When I came out, I found Jay in the den with his face buried in my phone. Looking a little closer, I saw tears falling from his eyes. What the hell was wrong with him? Did he get bad news from back home?

"What? What is it? Did something happen?" I asked with concern dripping from my voice. I was ready to break down crying right along with him.

"What the fuck is this sis?!" he asked as he turned the phone to face me. My heart plummeted because I never meant for anyone to see that video except me and Dallas. I never wanted to see that look my brother had on his face right now. "That nigga fuckin' raped you and you didn't bother to tell me?! You didn't tell me Tangi?!" Jay yelled with spit and snot spewing. I had never seen him so angry. "I done sat here and watched this video clip twice to make sure I wasn't trippin'..."

"Jay, stop!" I cried. "Yes! He did it and that's the main reason why I wanted to run away. I didn't know what he was gonna do next..."

"Let me tell you what he did next! That nigga came down to the fuckin' club and pulled a gun on me and Smooth! I should've lit his ass up then! I swear sis, if I would've known he hurt you like this, that nigga wouldn't be breathing now!" Jay handed me my phone and gave me a quick hug. "I'm so sorry sis. Sorry for not being there for you."

"No, it's my fault for not telling you how bad it was getting. I didn't think Dallas would go that far and when he did, I was lucky enough to have recorded that shit. That was the only way I was able to back him up off me long enough to fly up here."

"I honestly thought you were trippin' off you and Smooth breaking up then that shit with you and yo' girl Tierra…"

"It was that too, but mainly because of Dallas. He just wouldn't leave me alone."

"That's exactly why I'm about to fly my ass right back home!"

"No, don't go!"

Just as fast as my brother got here, he was ready to leave. "What? There ain't no way I'm not about to go back to Houston and handle that shit!"

"Please, you just got here!" I begged.

Jay gave in to me like always, but he didn't like it. Soon as his phone charged up, he was right on it making plans. I didn't know what he was up to, but I could bet my bottom dollar it had something to do with Dallas…

Waking up the next morning, I extended my body to an upright position and went in search of my brother.

Since I fell asleep early, I didn't know exactly which room Jay was staying in.

"What the hell?"

After checking every nook and cranny in that huge house, I discovered that my brother was gone. I should've known he was going to do that shit! He was going after Dallas.

Picking up the phone to call him, I kept getting his voicemail. He was either on the plane, had me blocked, or his cell was dead...and I knew darn well he hadn't blocked my number.

"Please don't let my brother do nothing stupid!" I prayed aloud as I went to my contact list. "Damn!"

It slipped my mind that I didn't have a number to call. I had deleted everyone out of my phone.

With no one to call to try to stop him, I got desperate and went online. "Fuck!"

Neither Smooth nor Jay had personal pages on social media. The only one they used was the public page created for the club and one of the staff members managed that shit.

"I give up!"

Starting to feel stressed, I freshened up, changed and went for a walk. Stepping outside, I bundled up and stretched my legs a bit before heading up the north trail.

Next, I put on my 'pump it up' playlist I had made to motivate me on my walks.

Sliding my earbuds in, I set out feeling pretty good. The walk was getting easier every day. I was even challenging myself by going a little farther each time.

"Hey!" I sang out as the song *'Talk'*, by Khalid came blasting in my ears. I got so into the song that I was throwing my hands in the air and even jogging a little.

Guess it was too much because before I knew it, I had twisted my ankle and went falling to the ground in excruciating pain. "Ouch! Fuck! Shit!" I cried clinching my lower leg.

Out in the middle of nowhere, I couldn't holler for help. My only choice was to pull myself up by the tree. That shit was hard as hell and took me three tries before I got on my feet, or should I say foot? Hobbling and placing all my weight on my right side, I could barely make it a few feet. I needed help.

Feeling embarrassed as I dialed emergency services, I had to tell them what happened. "So, I'm stuck out here and can't walk."

"Can you turn your location on?" she asked.

"Huh?"

"The location setting on your cell...can you turn that on for me so the medics can find you ma'am?" the female dispatcher asked.

Following her instructions, she was able to get an ambulance to me within 15 minutes. Not long after, I was arriving at Providence Hood River Memorial Hospital.

"Ma'am, we need to get you in for an X-ray to make sure you didn't break anything," the first doctor that saw me announced. "Is there any chance that you might be pregnant or..."

"No! Why is that even important?" I snapped defensively.

"I'm sorry, it's standard procedure to ask that question before giving an X-ray because it can cause harm to an unborn fetus..."

"Well, I'm not pregnant. At least not that I know of..."

"Ma'am, if there is the slightest chance..."

Shrugging my shoulders, I went ahead and gave them a urine sample. I didn't even think twice about the test coming back positive until that doctor pranced her ass back in there with a smile like she was delivering some good fucking news.

"Don't tell me! I'm pregnant?!" I frowned with my arms folded.

"Yes, looks like you are..."

"So, I can't have pain meds?! I can't have an X-ray!? Because if that's the damn case go head on and terminate this pregnancy right now!" I insisted with my bottom lip poked out.

"Now calm down ma'am," she urged with concern. "We just have to take special precautions with the x-ray, and we can give you something for the pain that won't harm the fetus."

Fuck! I was banking on these muthafuckas just terminating this shit! I can't have a baby! I don't deserve one after what the fuck I did the last time! Plus, I've been drinking and shit...

"Hey, I've been drinking kind of heavily these past couple of months. Can't that cause down syndrome and some mental disorders?" I asked curiously wondering if I fucked the kid up in my stomach without even knowing.

"We can possibly run some tests, but first let's get this ankle of yours checked out."

As I got myself taken care of, it began to sink in that I was pregnant again. This time felt different though.

What if it was Smooth's baby? Oh God! It just couldn't be Dallas' baby, could it? I mean, he did rape me! But he didn't ejaculate! But can I get pregnant by precum? Oh Lord, I just knew God wouldn't do this to me again.

My mind was in a whirl with questions and before I was released, I got as many answers as possible. They were needed in order for me to make my next decision which was, whether or not I was going to have this baby.

This is definitely something I need to pray about...

Please, please, please let this be Smooth's baby!

Chapter Eleven

Smooth

Jay ran off somewhere out of town to check on Tangi but ended up coming back to Houston the following day. He came and caught me down at the club.

"Nigga!" he snapped urging me to come to the office.

"What's up?" I asked with concern because right off I knew it was some shit.

Instead of telling me, he showed me a fucking two-minute video clip that he said he had forwarded from his sister's phone to his own. My eyes widened as I watched, and my heart ached when I saw what Dallas was doing to Tangi. I mean, she had mentioned something about that to me, but seeing it was worst. Then came the anger...

"Where that nigga at?!" I snapped snatching my heater out and cocking it back. That was how serious shit was getting. I was ready to find that fool and stop his breathing on sight!

That nigga had done so much shit to the woman that I loved. There was no way that I could let that shit go. I wasn't that kind of nigga.

"I don't know where that nigga is, but I suggest we start by looking for him at home," Jay said.

"Let's go then! It's time to lay that punk to rest!" So, we hopped in Jay's ride and headed to his new pad.

I don't give a fuck what he has to say. I'm just ready to put his ass to sleep with the maggots. I thought silently as we made it to his crib, but before we could pull into the driveway, I spotted a car parked there that I didn't recognize. I had Jay park across the street so we could chat for a minute.

"Yo, who car is that?" I asked Jay.

"I don't know, and I don't give a fuck! Shit, whoever is in there can get it too!" he said.

"Look man, nobody wants that nigga dead more than me, but we have to be rational about this. We can't just be killing people who have nothing to do with this."

"THAT NIGGA RAPED MY SISTER!!" he fumed looking like a mad dog! I mean, that nigga was foaming at the mouth and everything.

I already knew how protective he was when it came to his sister, but this was a totally different side of Jay that I had never seen. I was upset because of what that nigga had done to Tangi as well, but she wasn't my sister. It was different when it came to a bond between a brother and sister. At this point, it was up to me to bring that nigga down to earth. I couldn't lie though...it was like trying to reason with a mad man.

"I understand that, but we gotta go about this shit the right way. We can't just pop off on that nigga when he got company. I ain't trying to go to jail nigga!" I said.

"I want that nigga DEAD! Do you hear me?"

"I'm witchu bruh, but this just ain't the right time. We gotta do this some other time."

Jay gripped the steering wheel until his knuckles turned white then took several deep breaths before he pulled away. "That nigga gotta go... ya feel me?" Jay asked.

"I feel ya. Trust me, that nigga gonna get what's coming to him."

We headed back to the club where he parked his car and we went inside. No words were spoken about Dallas for the rest of the night. No words needed to be spoken because what was understood didn't need to be discussed any further.

I don't care how many fucked up decisions Tangi made! I ain't never gonna let a muthafucka do someone I love dirty like that. No, for shit like that...there has to be some consequences and repercussions!

8 days later...

Although I had been plotting on payback for Dallas' punk ass for the past week, I had been having Tangi heavy on my mind. I was just about to bug Jay about her that day in the bar, but out of the blue she came limping in.

Right off I wanted to ask her what happened, but her evil eye and the fact that she wasn't speaking prevented me from doing so. She hobbled right by and went to the office. My guess was that she was looking for her brother. I had missed her so much, so it was good to see her. My heart skipped several beats when I saw her. Just because she had gone missing didn't mean I didn't still love her.

I wondered what she and Jay were talking about, so I decided to barge in and find out. I was concerned about her, so I needed to check on her.

As I walked in, all conversations immediately stopped. Tangi looked me up and down and turned her attention back to her brother.

"Did you do this?" she asked Jay.

"Do what?" he asked.

"Did you or you," she asked as she looked at me. "Have something to do with this man's disappearance?"

"What man? Jay, what's she talking about?" I asked.

"Man, that fool Dallas done got his ass missing somewhere, so she thinks I had something to do with that shit!" Jay said as he rolled his eyes and ran his hand down his face.

"Oh, don't act like y'all didn't know he was missing! I was all the way out of state, and I saw his mom begging for his safe return on the national news!" She then turned back to Jay and asked, "Come on bro, you can tell me anything. Did you do something?"

"I don't know what you talking about sis. I been working my ass off at the club. I don't know shit about that nigga..."

"Was it you?" she asked me as she leaned onto the desk for support.

"Was it me what?"

"Did you do something to Dallas?"

"I ain't do shit to that nigga! I ain't even seen that muthafucka since he tried to shoot me last week!" I said.

"I wonder what happened to him then," she pondered.

"Why do you care?!" I asked. "I mean, after what that muthafucka did to you, he deserves to rot in hell!!"

"That's not for either of you to decide! Only God can judge!" she said. "And Jay, last time you and I spoke, you were determined to get even with Dallas. So, you can imagine how I felt when I saw that he was missing!"

"Yea, but you can relax because I ain't did shit to that nigga. He probably just needed some space like you did..."

"Or his ass is hiding because he knows he done pissed a bunch of people off!" I said.

"Maybe. But y'all better hope that y'all didn't do nothing to that man because he ain't worth y'all going to jail for!" Tangi said as she eyed both of us.

"Ain't nobody going to jail Tangi..." I said.

"Right, cuz we ain't did shit!" Jay finished.

"Alright. Y'all better hope not," she said as she limped out.

I rushed behind her because I needed to talk to her. I caught up with her before she got in the car. "Tangi!"

She stopped and looked at me. "What? I'm not in the mood for no bullshit from you tonight. I just got off the plane and I'm tired as fuck!"

"Why it gotta be all that? I miss you. I just wanted to make sure you were okay," I said speaking from the heart. "I see you hurt your leg..."

"It's my ankle and I'm fine. Just a little jetlag..."

"What happened? Where were you?"

"None of your business Smooth. We ain't together no more, so what I do doesn't concern you," she said rudely.

"Damn! Why you so uptight?"

"Uptight? I'm uptight?" she asked.

"You never used to speak to me this way..."

"Well, get used to it or leave me alone. Look, I'd like to continue this shit, but I gotta go. Like I said, I'm exhausted," she huffed filled with irritation.

"Can we meet up for coffee or something, so we can talk?" I asked.

"I don't know. I'll let you know."

Tangi got in the car and left before I could respond. Things between us were definitely strained, but I hoped to change that.

Shaking my head in defeat, I headed back inside to talk to Jay. I had nothing but his sister on my mind.

Call me crazy, but I still wanna be with Tangi...

Chapter Twelve

Tierra

As I sat in the rocker feeding Miracle while watching television, I couldn't believe that Dallas' mother had reported him missing. Where the hell was that fool? He was probably hiding out somewhere hoping to get some attention from Tangi. Dumb ass.

As I listened to his mom begging for him to come home or call her to let her know that he was okay, my heart broke for her. I couldn't imagine what I'd be going through if anything like that happened to Miracle. She was my only child and the love of my life. The love a mother felt for her child was something no one else could understand unless they were a mom.

Dallas hadn't always been the best husband, but at one time we were good friends. I never would want anything bad to happen to him, even though he probably deserved it. At the end of the day, he was still Miracle's father.

To hear her pleas clearly, I turned the volume up to listen to what Momma Armstrong was saying.

"Dallas baby, if you can hear me, please come home! If you have seen my son or have any information about his

disappearance, please, please contact the police department. And if you did something to my son, God has a special place for you!" She began to cry as the reporter began speaking into the microphone again.

"Dallas Armstrong has been missing for five days now. If you have any information concerning Mr. Armstrong's whereabouts, you are encouraged to contact the Houston Police Department. Back to you Ron..."

The segment then switched to the newscaster in the newsroom. As I drew my attention away from the news, I wondered where Dallas was. I didn't even know he was missing until the detectives showed up on my doorstep a couple of days ago. That shit still had me rattled because they might've thought I had something to do with his disappearance.

Hell, I'd probably be a suspect if I hadn't given birth recently.

BANG! BANG! BANG!

I had just closed my eyes for a much needed nap when the banging on the door woke me up. I stretched and made my way to the door to answer it. Whoever it was, they were banging on my damn door like the fucking police.

Imagine my surprise when I opened the door and it was the police on the other side. "Ms. Armstrong, I'm

Detective Peters and this is my partner Detective Martinez. We'd like to ask you some questions concerning your ex-husband Dallas Armstrong. May we come in?"

I stepped to the left to allow them to come inside. "I don't know what this is about, but whatever they said he did, he probably did it!" I blurted out without thinking first.

"You sound like you have some hostility where your ex is concerned," Detective Peters stated.

"Well, he did threaten to shoot me a couple of weeks ago, soooooo..."

"Tell us about that," Detective Peters requested.

"What is this about? Why are you here?" I asked.

"As I said, we're here to ask you questions about your ex..."

"But why? Why are you asking me questions about Dallas? I mean, we're divorced."

"Well, Ms. Armstrong, your ex-husband has been reported missing..."

"Missing? Who reported him missing?" I asked playing dumb for no reason. Hell, I had just seen the shit on TV! I guess my nervousness made me jump to the defensive side.

"It was his mother who reported him missing."

"Wow! Well, knowing Dallas, he's probably just off somewhere seeking attention!" I said.

"Nonetheless, we still have to question those who were associated with him," Detective Martinez stated.

"See, that's where you're barking up the wrong tree. I haven't been associated with him since we divorced."

"But didn't you just give birth to his daughter a couple of months ago?"

"Yea, so?"

"So, doesn't he see his child?" Detective Peters pressed like she was hinting around to something.

"I have a TRO against my ex following the incident where he threatened my life."

"When did that happen?" Detective Martinez asked as she jotted some shit down in her little black spiral notepad.

"For detectives, you guys sure didn't do your jobs investigating. I mean, you could've easily looked all that information up before you got here... unless you already knew this shit and you're harassing me to see if there's anything more to it. Well, let me save y'all some of y'all's precious time..." I said as I walked over to the kitchen drawer where I kept the restraining order papers. I handed them to the detective and stood with my arms across my chest. I mean, they're detectives who don't do their damn jobs. I wonder if the chief knew about the way they were handling things.

"Here!" I huffed with irritation.

Taking their own sweet time, the two of them looked at the paperwork before handing it back to me. "When was the last time you saw your ex-husband?"

"The night he showed up here drunk and threatening to shoot me!" I repeated.

"And you haven't seen him since?" Detective Martinez asked as he peered at me.

"What part of no don't you understand? I haven't seen or heard from him and I don't care to either. Look, wherever Dallas is I'm sure he's getting a kick out of watching all this shit unfold. I'm sure he's fine and just waiting on the right time to make his presence known. In case no one informed y'all, my ex-husband is an attention whore! He does shit strictly to get people's attention... period!"

Even though I sounded like I was talking a good game, I was scared as fuck. The last thing I wanted was to be accused of having something to do with why they couldn't find Dallas' ass. I didn't know where he was or what his motive for doing this shit was, but he had better let these people know that he was okay. That shit didn't make any sense to me at all.

"Well, thank you for your time Ms. Armstrong. If you should hear from your ex-husband..."

"I won't!"

"As I was saying, if you should hear from Mr. Armstrong please tell him to contact the police department," Detective Peters said.

"If I should hear from my ex, I will be contacting the police department because he's not supposed to contact me!" I stated before the two of them handed me their business cards and headed for the door.

When they left, I didn't call Thaddeus to tell him about my unexpected visit from the cops. I waited for him to come home, so that I could make his plate and get him in front of the TV just in time for the local news to come on.

It took less than ten minutes before a picture of Dallas finally popped up. Immediately glancing over at Thaddeus as he ate dinner, I noticed that he didn't seem shocked or anything by the news.

"You know the police came by to see me earlier?" I said as I watched his reaction from a sideways glance.

"About what?" he asked as he continued to eat his food, unbothered in the least.

"About Dallas' disappearance!"

"Why did they wanna talk to you?"

"Because I'm his ex-wife... DUH! I mean, they wanted to know when was the last time I had seen him or if I had heard from him recently."

That was a stupid question.

"What'd you tell them?" he probed in between bites.

"I told them that I hadn't spoken to or seen him since the night he came over here to threaten me. I also showed them the restraining order and told them that if he did contact me, they would be the first ones I'd call," I said.

"Damn right! That nigga knows better than to bring his ass around here again!" He continued eating his food as if he didn't care that Dallas was missing.

That had me looking at him differently, and I had been looking at him that way ever since. I didn't want to believe that Thaddeus had anything to do with Dallas going missing, but shit, anything was possible...

Two days went by and still no word from Dallas. As I sat home reflecting on everything that had been happening lately, I began to think about how Thaddeus took the news when I told him about Dallas being missing. His actions that day had me eyeing him suspiciously. I mean, he couldn't have had anything to do with Dallas' disappearance, right?

"Let me not drive myself crazy about this shit!" I chanted aloud as I went to check on Miracle.

When I stepped into the empty room, my heart dropped until I remembered that Thaddeus had taken her with him to his brother's house. I really didn't want him to take her, but they were having a birthday party over there for his niece. Plus, I needed some rest. I hadn't been sleeping well since I found out Dallas was missing.

BAM! BAM! BAM!

"Who the hell could that be?!" I complained under my breath as I went to answer the door looking a hot mess. My hair was all over my head and I was dressed only in some boy shorts and a tube top.

Swinging the door back with a major attitude, I saw Momma Armstrong standing there with her arms folded and tears in her eyes. I wanted to go off, but my heart wouldn't let me. After all, her son was missing. I had no choice but to invite her in...

"So, I know I shouldn't have just stopped by here like this but I'm desperate Tierra! I know you've seen the news..."

"Yes, and I wanted to reach out to you, but I didn't have your number." I said knowing that I deleted that shit once she came over acting a fool.

"My number is the same, but I see yours ain't. I tried it several times," she said a little snappy, but not enough to make me flip on her. I knew how to choose my battles wisely.

"Okay, so where are they at with the investigation?" I asked ignoring her remark and going on with the conversation.

"Investigation?!" she shrieked as she dried her face with a wad of used tissue. "You think the cops are out there looking for a missing *black man* Tierra?!"

"Well..."

"Well, hell!" she snapped angrily. "The only black men the police are out there looking for are the ones with warrants or ones walking down the street minding their own damn business! That does not include my son! No one cares if he's been missing for almost a damn week! No one is looking for him Tierra!"

Now, Momma Armstrong went on and on about Dallas and her emotions were all over the place. She went from crying to yelling.

"I don't even know why I came here Tierra! You obviously don't give a damn about my son..."

"That's not true! We may not see eye to eye, but I'd never wish that any real harm to come to him Momma Armstrong!" I tried to convince her, knowing that I had been wishing bad on Dallas since the day I found out that he was fucking Tangi!

But never... never for him to just go missing! I couldn't imagine what might have happened to him...

Chapter Thirteen

Mrs. Armstrong

Sick of hearing a million and one excuses from Tierra, I stood up and went off. I didn't mean to, but I was at my wits end.

"Look Tierra, stop playing the fucking victim! You know good and damn well you don't give a shit about my son!" I snapped clutching my handbag to let her know I was a pistol packing grandma. I didn't know what the hell she was up to!

"Oh, so now you cursing me in my own house?!" she huffed getting up boldly to face me, only she was about four inches shorter and 30 pounds lighter. She may have shoved me the last time, but I was ready for her ass this time around!

"Yes, the hell I am!" I yelled down at her. "Dallas just didn't up and vanish into thin fuckin' air. You can sit up here all you want and act like…"

"Get out!"

"What the fuck…"

"You heard me… GET OUT OF MY HOUSE!! This time don't bring your ass back!" she hollered rushing by me to gesture me out. "If you do, you better hope the cops get you first!"

"As a matter of fact, let me help you out..." She started before her man sized little boy toy came in with my grandbaby in the stroller. He parked it near the sofa then jumped in between us and began trying to check me.

"Don't come up in our house with that bullshit!" he shouted with his disrespectful ass. No good upbringing and he was trying to challenge me! He may have been a little taller than I was, but my chest was certainly bigger than his. I used it to push him off me long enough to make it to the other side of the door. That's when I began talking shit.

"I knew you two had something to do with my son's disappearance and I'm gonna prove that shit! Neither of you liked him and it would be much more convenient for your man to play daddy with Dallas out of the way! Then you two could be the perfect little fucking family!" I yelled out crying.

"That's where you're wrong!" Tierra hollered back as he held onto the edge of the door. "We already are the perfect fucking family! Now get the hell off my property!"

Slamming it before I could get another word out, she nearly caught my foot in the door. When I snatched it out of the way, I tumbled backwards and fell against the siderail. Now I was really mad. I wanted to go back in there and whoop Tierra's ass! She was damn lucky that my grandbaby was in there! Yeah, so was her new dude, but I wasn't worried about his ass! I had fought bigger and badder men than him in my day.

Feeling fed up and exhausted, I left there as the sun began to set and went to Dallas' house. I hadn't been in there since I went with the cops to do a welfare check. They said I wasn't allowed in after that, but I had left the back door unlocked especially so I could go back.

When I got there, my hands were trembling. Unlike the last time, the air was eerie and gave me an uneasy feeling inside.

Chill bumps began rising on my limbs as I climbed from my car and went through the back gate. The darkness made it nearly impossible to tread the covered trail that led to the backyard. Waiting until I felt safe enough, I drew out my cell and used the flashlight to help find my way through the sliding door and into the kitchen.

"What the hell?" I gasped as I saw miscellaneous shit strewn about the house. It definitely wasn't like that when I was there with the cops a day before!

Thinking the worse, all of a sudden, I heard a big bang that came from the kitchen. I was so startled that I drew my gun out and took two shots toward where the noise came from.

"What the hell was I thinking?" I panicked as I put my gun in my purse and ran out of the front door, leaving it wide open. I was just sure the cops were coming after I shot off those loud blasts.

My hands shook uncontrollably as I flew outside while checking to see if any neighbors were coming out. "My ass is in trouble! Why did I do that dumb shit?"

Being that I was almost 50, I was way too old to be running from the damn police. I had to be smart and get away while I still had the chance. I thought I was free and clear, until I noticed someone taking pictures of me coming out of the house.

Why my dumb ass didn't see the white van sitting there parked across the street was beyond me. What gave them away was the glare from the streetlight into their window. That presented a clear view of the man dressed in black that was taking the pics.

What am I gonna do now? Should I just wait for the cops?! I mean, I wasn't doing shit! It wasn't like I would kill or hurt my own son! They had to know that!

Looking down at my skin, I knew that the odds were against me. I would take my chances and run. At least I would live and be free another day.

The only way I could see myself getting out of this one was to catch the person responsible for my son being missing. Tierra and her boyfriend were my only leads. Since neither of them was coming clean about knowing anything, I had to go in another direction. I had to go to my son's job.

That night I went home, but the next morning I got up bright and early and went to Dallas' office. There were only a few people working, but I knew at least one of them, Carl.

Casually going over to him, he greeted me with a hug. "Ms. Armstrong, how are you? Haven't seen you here in years..."

"Yeah, I never really had a reason to come by until now."

"You still haven't heard from Dallas?" Carl whispered pulling me to the side for privacy.

"No! It's been days and I'm really worried about him. It's not like him to just take off and not keep in touch with me. Has he been having any trouble that you know of?"

"Well, if you wanna count all those times he got his ass... I mean... if you want to count the time some guy came up here and jumped on Dallas? Or the time he came to work with a black eye?" Carl said trying to hold in his laugh. I didn't know why that shit was so hard for him to do. It wasn't funny to me at all! My fucking son was missing!

"Look Carl! Spare me the dramatics and tell me who the man was that came up here fighting my son!" I insisted as I stared him down with a serious expression.

"I think I heard him call the dude Jay. I've never seen him before, but he looked pretty tough. Like a thug." He then went on to describe the man from head to toe.

"And that's all you know Carl?" I asked suspiciously. "I know how you men talk in this office. Just like athletes talk in the locker room! You know something!"

"Look, all I know is that Dallas was messing with the dude's sister. And that's why he came up here and handled him. He told Dallas to stay the hell away from his sister and walked out."

"Did you call the police?" I asked.

"Why would I do that? He was still alive and all. I mean, he had a black eye and busted lip, but if he wanted to call the police, he would've done that himself. That's all I know and I gotta go. But, I hope you hear from your son soon. We need him to run this office." Carl said before leaving me standing there.

I stood there wondering who the hell that Jay was that was fighting with my son. Why hadn't Dallas told me about that? I then pondered on the idea of whether he could be the reason my son was missing. But who the hell was he?

"Tangi!" I whispered under my breath as it hit me. I knew she had a brother named Jay, but I had no idea where to find either of their asses. Honestly, I didn't even know where to start looking.

Not being the social network butterfly, I barely had a Facebook page and definitely didn't know how to work it. All I could do was sign in and scroll through the newsfeed. I did that shit for a good 20 minutes before I thought of someone who knew all about it... my nephew Todd.

Dialing him up, I gave him all the information I had. "Auntie, I'll get back to you in the hour. I should have something for you then." Todd assured and kept true to his word.

Half an hour later, he was calling me back giving me a big piece of news. Tangi's brother Jay owned a club on the other side of town.

"I guess I got somewhere to dress up and go to tonight!" I laughed wickedly as I went to my closet and started going through my wardrobe.

Oh, it's on tonight! Either somebody was gon' tell me something or I was gon' wreck shop on that ass!

Chapter Fourteen

Smooth

"Did you find your glove that you dropped over at that niggas house?" Jay pressed when I met him up at the club the following night.

"I went back over there looking for the shit and somebody came in while I was inside!"

"What the fuck?!" Jay whispered with a frown. "Did they see you?"

"Nah, a nigga almost got busted though. I hid in the pantry and tried to wait until the person was gone, but then my clumsy ass knocked over some boxes of cereal and cans and shit. I guess it scared the bitch as much as it scared me because she shot two rounds then ran out the front!" I told him.

"How the fuck you know it was a 'she'?"

"Because I had lil Sammie with me and that nigga was lucky enough to catch the chick flying out the door and took some pics of her, and her car!"

"Do you know who she is?"

"Yeah, ran the bitch's plates and come to find out, she's Dallas' mother!"

"What the fuck she doin' over there with a gun? She gotta suspect something!"

"It don't matter because we got her ass flying from the scene of a shooting and so did some of the neighbors! The cops came and everything!"

As Jay and I were discussing what had happened, his cell began to ring. He held up his finger and answered it.

"Hey sis, what's up?"

Of course, now that Tangi was back in town, she still wasn't talking to me. She wasn't staying at her house, so I figured that she had been at her brother's. Only I didn't want to ask him and seem pressed, especially since we had a lot of shit going on.

That nigga Dallas was missing and me and Jay knew that we would be on the list of suspects. We not only had a major beef with the nigga and whooped his ass, but we had gone over there the day of his disappearance to confront him about the video clip. We wanted that nigga dead for what he had done to Tangi. I mean, what nigga claimed they loved a woman then turned around and raped her? For that shit, he deserved to have his fucking block knocked off.

That nigga acted as though he was invincible or something. When Tangi barged up in here accusing us of some shit, I thought she might have found some evidence on us. But she was just checking our asses because she knew we disliked the dude. Hell, we weren't the only niggas in this city who disliked that muthafucka! The list was long as well with people who didn't like his ass! I mean, me and Jay didn't like him, Tangi didn't like him, and I bet at the top of that list was Tierra and her man. I mean, Dallas had fucked over her more than any other person that I know.

I mean, he had fucked Tierra's best friend, left her while she was pregnant, and threatened to kill her ass. I found out about that from a lil tip from my friend who worked at the police station. He informed me that Tierra had a restraining order on that nigga after he showed up at her crib in the middle of the night with a gun. Shit, I wouldn't have even gotten the police involved in that shit. I would've killed his ass on sight. She had surveillance so it would've been self- defense.

Some of these women were pathetic. They claimed to be independent and shit but couldn't do the right thing when it fell right in their damn laps. She could've killed that nigga without any consequences because he came on her property with a gun, but she didn't. And that coward ass bodybuilder she was dating didn't do shit either. I sure hoped they never find that nigga.

Like I said, too many people wanted his ass dead. When Jay hung up the phone, I asked, "How's Tangi?"

"She's cool. Her ankle is better, but she's been a little under the weather since she got back, but I think it has to do with the sudden climate change. Where she was it was freezing ya know? And then she comes back here, and she's hit with all this heat."

"So, where was she?" I asked. I mean, he seemed to be in a telling mood so...

"Ha Ha! You still fishing me for information huh? I already told you that I ain't giving up none of my sister's business. If she wanted you to know where she was she would've told you already," Jay clowned.

"Well, besides her ankle, what's wrong with her?"

"What do you mean?"

"Well, you said she's been under the weather since she's been back. What's wrong with her?" I asked.

"I'on know. She's just a lil sluggish, ya know, tired and stuff. She even threw up a couple of times. I told her she was out there for a good while, so her body has to get used to being back in the south. She'll be fine in a few days," he said.

"I hope so. I mean, she's been back over a week. Maybe she should get checked out by the doctor. She might have some kind of virus."

I was concerned about her. Maybe I'd leave a little early and drop by her crib to cook her some soup or something. I mean, soup cures everything, right? At least that's what my mom and grandmother would say. Jay and I continued to chop it up until the woman from the pics showed up. Dallas' mother!

"Oh, oh," I remarked. "Trouble at twelve o'clock."

"What trouble?" Jay asked as his eyes looked toward the door. "What now?"

"That's the woman from the other night! That's Dallas' momma!" I whispered.

The woman was now standing there chatting with the security guard before he pointed to the two of us. I just knew for some reason she was going to be headed our way. I prayed she wouldn't make a scene or cause any problems because I wasn't scared to have a woman thrown out on her ass.

A couple of minutes later, she stepped up to the two of us. "Which one of you niggas here named Jay?"

Jay stood straight up, towering over her by several inches. "I'm Jay. What can I do for you?" he asked.

"I wanna know why you was at my son's office getting in his ass!"

Shit, I almost choked on my damn drink at her brazen attitude. She obviously wasn't the least bit intimidated by Jay's size.

"First of all, who is your son?" Jay asked.

"Oh, so you just go around beating niggas up all the time, huh?" the lady asked.

"Perhaps we should take this in my office," Jay suggested calmly.

"Whatever!"

The two of them headed toward the office with me following behind them. The woman stopped abruptly and turned to me. "What the hell are you following us for?"

"I'm his partner..."

"I don't give a shit what you are! Unless your name is Jay, I ain't got shit for you!" she said rudely.

"Ma'am as I said before, I'm his business partner so..."

"Well, go partner your ass over there and find you some business because I ain't got none for you!" she barked as she held her purse tightly.

Figuring she had a heater inside, I decided to step back and wait for my boy's signal. I wasn't budging until he gave me the greenlight.

"I'll be fine," Jay said.

"Shit, I came to talk... PERIODT!! If you need a bodyguard for a conversation, you must be a wimp or punk!"

"I'm neither and we can have a conversation in my office," Jay said.

The woman rolled her eyes at me and turned to follow behind Jay. I pretended to turn the other way, but I followed them to the office. That lil woman was feisty as fuck and packing, so there was no way I was going to allow Jay to get shot up or something like that. I stood outside the door and tried to listen to the conversation.

"What can I do for you ma'am?" asked Jay.

"I told you that I wanna know why you went to fight my son at his office!"

"Ma'am what happened between me and your son was between us. I went to speak with him about something, we hashed it out and that was that..."

"You went to speak to him about your whoring ass sista..."

"Hey, you gon' watch your mouth when you talk about my sister!"

"Or what?" she asked. "She knew my son was married to HER BEST FRIEND!! Yet she still didn't hesitate to drop her lil funky ass draws for him. What you think that make her? She sho' ain't no damn saint!"

"My sister may not be a saint, but she's definitely not a whore..."

"I beg to differ!" Dallas' mom snapped nastily. Shit, I knew that Jay was getting hot under the collar on that one. That nigga hated when people, anybody, talked about Tangi. In his eyes, she could do no wrong. "Your sister is a straight up whore for fuckin' her best friend's husband! Now, I know you might think highly of your baby sister, so you would never say no shit like that... but hell, I'm sure you thought it."

"Ma'am, I'm gonna have to ask you to leave. I won't allow you to stand in here and disrespect my sister!"

"I ain't going nowhere until you tell me if you had something to do with my son's disappearance!" She insisted with her hands on her hips and her wig sitting sideways on the top of her head.

"I ain't had shit to do with his disappearance! But I ain't gon' lie to you though. Wherever his ass is, he'd better stay there after what he did to my sister!"

"And what the hell does that mean? What did he supposedly do to your sister? Last I heard, they were both messing around and doing it to each other!"

That shit had me fuming, so I know damn well Jay was mad as fuck where he was. That ol' lady was coming at him with insults left and right about Tangi. I knew he was talking about Dallas raping Tangi, but the last thing we needed was for him to tell that woman about it and then she run to the cops and give them a motive for the two of them to want his ass dead. Nah, he needed to keep his mouth shut and that shit to himself.

"Ma'am, I don't know where your son is! I haven't seen him since the day I beat his ass and warned him to stay away from my sister. As far as I knew, he had kept away from her, so we didn't have any other problems.

Now, if you'll excuse me, I got some work to do." Jay summarized.

"I wonder what the police would think about your little spat with my son. I mean, they ain't came by to talk to you yet, so maybe I need to have a talk with those detectives and send them your way. You've obviously been hiding some shit and holding on to some resentment for my son. You need to tell the police about it," the woman urged with a bad attitude.

"Lady, I just told you that I ain't had shit to do with your son's disappearance!"

"Then tell it to the cops! I'm also gonna let them know to investigate your slu... oops, I mean, sister! She obviously got some lil secret she's hiding and that might have to do with why my son is missing!" she said.

"Lady, for the last time, we..."

"Yea, yea, yea!! We'll see what the cops have to say about all that shit!" I could hear her voice getting closer to the door, so I jetted around the corner and took a seat at the bar. She was not gonna come out that office barking at my ass. I didn't need any more trouble from her ass.

She rushed by me, then stopped and made her way over to where I sat. "Excuse me, what'd you say your name was?" she asked.

"I didn't."

"Well, what is it?" she asked with her lips in a tight straight line.

"Why do you need to know my name?" I asked.

"Oh, well, before you was all sticking your chest out and shit talking about you Mr. Business Partner and all and now you won't give me your name! Humph!" she said as she eyed me up and down. "The police might need to speak to you also. It's cool, you ain't gotta give me your damn name. Mr. Business Partner." For every word she said, she wrote in her lil pad with a pen.

When she was done, she looked up at me and smiled. "I'll send the police to question yo big fine ass too!" With that, she turned on her heels and walked out the door. What the hell was up with that woman?

Why the hell was she trying to get my ass locked up for some bullshit?! She didn't know shit about me but was still trying to lock my ass up behind some bullshit with her raggedy ass son!

I ain't going to jail! That much I know...

Chapter Fifteen

Tangi

Dallas had been missing for a good two weeks now. Shit, I was glad ain't nobody bothered me about that shit because I didn't know where that asshole was. I was just glad that he had finally stopped bothering me about getting back together. The last thing I wanted was to be anywhere near his ass. I was so done with Dallas Armstrong. I didn't know what I had seen in him in the first place.

KNOCK! KNOCK! KNOCK!

I looked at the clock on the cable box and saw that it was almost seven. I wasn't expecting anyone, but it was probably Jay coming by to check on me. He knew I wasn't feeling well and suggested that it might be due to the climate change. Little did my big brother know it was because I was pregnant. I was shocked beyond reason to find out that it happened again so soon.

Yeah, I thought about getting rid of the baby, but knew darn well there was no way I was going through that again. Besides, this baby was made out of my love for Smooth. Just because he and I weren't in a good place right now didn't mean he wouldn't be an excellent father to our child. I knew that he loved me, and I loved him. I was just pissed at how he practically forced me to come clean to Tierra. If it hadn't been for that discussion we were having that Tierra overheard, she and I would still be the best of friends.

Now, she had a baby whose life I couldn't even be a part of. Even though we had promised each other to be godmothers to each other's children way back in the day. I missed my friend. And now that I was having a baby of my own, I missed her more than ever. It was really lonely not having anyone to talk to besides my mother and brother. I made my way to the door to let Jay in.

I pulled the door back and there stood my baby's daddy with a couple of bags in his hand. My heartbeat quickened at the sight of him. I was super excited to see him, but of course I wasn't about to let him see that.

"Hey," he greeted.

"Hey."

"Can I come in?"

"What are you doing here Smooth?" I asked after I had let him in.

"Well, your brother kind of let on that you weren't feeling well. I thought I'd come by and make you some of my grandmother's homemade soup. She always said it could cure anything," he said with a hopeful smile.

Not anything.

"That was nice, but I really don't feel..."

"Look Tangi, I know shit between us has been real fucked up. For my part that I played in it, I apologize. I mean that from the bottom of my heart. I never meant to hurt you or anything like that. But I know that by you holding on to that secret was killing you. I'm sorry shit between you and Tierra fell apart too. I really am."

The look on his face was so sincere and genuine. It made me want to cry, but I wasn't going to do that. There was no reason for me to break down and cry like a pussy. I just continued to stand there looking at him.

"Look, I just came by to check on you and make you some soup. If you want me to go, I'll go."

I didn't answer for a couple of minutes, so he grabbed the bags, and headed for the door. "Wait!" I called before he could open it. Shit, this man was offering to cook a homemade meal for me. What the hell was wrong with me? "You can stay."

Smooth turned around towards me with the biggest smile on his face. "All you have to do is relax and let me take care of the rest," he assured as he set the bags down and went to work.

Watching him do all that for me made my heart overflow with love for him. Dallas had never cooked for me once. We never even went out anywhere because we couldn't afford for anyone to see us and tell Tierra. To be honest, all we ever did was have sex. He paid a few of my bills, but to be honest and bought me some cheap gifts, but it was nothing like what I had with Smooth. Smooth was the real deal and I was about to throw it all away because of my friendship with Tierra going to pieces.

Looking at this sexy, handsome man prepare a meal for me melted any ice that was around my heart. I couldn't continue blaming him for some shit that I had done. I ruined my friendship with Tierra, not him or anyone else. I had been blaming him and it wasn't his doing. He didn't force me to sleep with Dallas. I did that fucked up shit on my own. All Smooth was trying to do was get me to see how much keeping that secret was hurting me.

"How did you learn how to cook that?" I inquired as I sat down on the barstool.

"My grandmother taught me how to cook this. She taught me how to cook a lot," he said with a smile.

"How come you never cooked for me before?"

"I planned to one day, but then shit happened that kind of fucked us up, ya know?"

"Yea, I know. I owe you an apology for the way I overreacted and blamed you," I confessed.

"Whaaaaat?" he teased. "If I had known food was gon' get you to apologize, I would've come by to cook for you a long time ago."

"Shut up!" I teased back. "No, but seriously, I was wrong. I should've taken responsibility for the part I played in what happened. I never should've put that blame on your shoulders because you had nothing to do with it."

I suddenly felt the overwhelming need to vomit. Jumping off the barstool, I took off for the bathroom and made it just in time to throw my face into the toilet bowl and empty the contents of my stomach. It was like as soon as he put the beef meat in the pot, my tummy started bubbling. A couple of seconds later, I felt my hair gently being pulled to the back as Smooth stroked my back.

"Are you okay?" he asked when I was done.

Smooth then wet a towel and handed it to me. I wiped my face and mouth before grabbing the toothpaste and toothbrush. After brushing my teeth, I gurgled with mouthwash. Then I looked at him and nodded.

"I'm fine."

We walked back to the kitchen where he filled a glass with ice and water and handed it to me. I sat back on the barstool and sipped on the water while he resumed his cooking. "Thanks," I said.

"You're welcome."

I thought about telling him about the baby, but I didn't know how. I mean, I couldn't just blurt it out now could I? It just didn't seem like now was the right time.

"I think I'm just gonna go lay down until you're finish. I'm feeling a lil lightheaded," I admitted as I slid off the stool and sighed.

Coming quickly to my side, Smooth laced his arm with mine and helped me to my bed. He allowed me to lean on him as we headed down the hallway. Once in my room, he tucked me in and everything. It sure felt nice having him take care of me this way. I really had missed him, and I still loved him with all my heart.

"Can you hand me that remote please?" I requested.

Once I had it in hand and Smooth left out of the room, I turned the TV on and began watching the local news. I wanted to see if there was any word concerning Dallas' whereabouts.

Trying my best to stay awake, I cut the volume up and fluffed the pillow behind my head. That only made it worse.

As the comfort of the pillowtop mattress beneath my body enveloped me, my eyes slowly closed. Now lost in a deep sleep, visions of Smooth and I danced in my head.

"Mmmmm!" I hummed as I imagined his lips against mine.

Suddenly I heard an echo. There was humming...

"Let me stop before you get me sick too." Smooth laughed as he pecked my mouth a few more times before backing up and serving my food to me on a tray. He even picked up the damn spoon and started feeding me.

Blowing on the soup, he smiled and gestured me to open my mouth. Feeling too tickled, I opened up and accepted the bite of the delicious soup. Oh God! It was so good!

"This is really good!" I mumbled.

"Thanks. I haven't made it in a long time, so I wasn't sure if I still had my touch," he bragged as he sat beside me talking and taking care of me until the television caught both of our attention.

"We're down here on the steps of the Houston Police Department where we have a very worried mother here seeking help in finding her son Dallas Armstrong, who has been missing now for several weeks.

We need the whole community in on this one..."

"That's Dallas' mother... right there on TV hosting a damn rally!" I screeched as I heard her going off about the cops not being out there searching for her son. She was hollering about if it were a white man that was missing... ya know, playing the race card.

"Yeah, she came up to the club earlier and went off on me and your brother. She's a damn fool!"

"You'd be a damn fool too if your child was missing!" I snapped and immediately regretted it once I saw the sadness in Smooth's eyes. I knew he had to be thinking about the child we lost.

Damn, this is the perfect time to tell him about the pregnancy. But what if he doesn't want it? Do I even wanna chance it?

Nah, I didn't. I wasn't ready.

"Give me a second baby. Let me get this stuff outta here," Smooth whispered as he slid his arm off my shoulder and got up to gather the dishes. "You want something from the kitchen while I'm going in there?"

"Yeah, can you bring me some orange juice on ice, please?" I requested as I snuggled back down into my bed.

As Smooth disappeared, I began thinking about a way to come out and tell him about the pregnancy. It was hard to share such news because I still wasn't sure how I felt about it.

Let me just go get these papers and hand them to him when he comes back in the room.

Rising to my feet, I went to my dresser and opened it. "Dammit! Now, where did I put those papers?"

Standing there thinking as hard as I could, I tried to remember where I last had the documents that the doctor gave me at the hospital. Then it came to me. I had them earlier that day when I made my appointment at the OB clinic. "Damn, I left them on the kitchen counter!"

Recalling just where I placed them, I ran in there only to find them gone and Smooth too. He even left the door wide open.

Hurrying to get my cell, I pulled up my contacts to call him like a damn dummy! I had deleted his number!

What now?

There was nothing that I could do about the shit, so I would deal with that when Smooth came to me with it. Until then, there was something else that I had to deal with. That rally that was going on at the police station.

Throwing on some clothes, I headed down there only to find a larger crowd than I had expected. The first person I ran into was Momma Armstrong.

"Tangi!" she gasped as she came within arm's reach and slapped me. "Why the hell would you come here when it's all your fault that my son is missing!"

Just as I was about to strike that bitch back, Tierra came from nowhere and stood between us. "Get your fuckin' hands off her!"

"You shut the hell up! Y'all both probably in on this together!" Momma Armstrong yelled before a uniformed cop escorted her away from us.

"Thank you, Tierra." I smiled astonished that she took up for me.

"No thanks needed. That bitch is out of control!" she smirked and began to walk away.

"Wait!" I called as I quickly fell in step with her. "Can we talk?" I pressed hoping to get her to say yes.

"No! I still ain't got shit to say to you Tangi. The only reason why I stepped in was because I really can't stand that bitch!" She frowned then looked me up and down. "Now that I think about it... I'm still not too fond of your ass either."

Throwing her nose in the air, she walked off in the opposite direction leaving me standing there looking stupid. At least that was how I was feeling...

Chapter Sixteen

Mrs. Armstrong

First Tangi, then Tierra's funky ass. I should've whooped them both. Them little bitches tried to tag team me too! Yeah, they had it coming!

"Could you let my arm loose?" I snapped at the cop that was still detaining me for slapping the piss out of Tangi.

"Ma'am, you need to calm down or leave the premises..."

"This is a public place and I can stand where the hell I want to! Do you even care that this rally is going on because MY SON is missing?!" I demanded as he pulled out the cuffs and dangled them in my face.

That clue straightened my ass right on up. I couldn't afford to be locked up while my son was missing. I needed to be out there looking for him. Just like the lazy ass cops needed to be doing instead of holding me up.

"Can I go now, please?" I requested in a pleasant tone. I had to put myself on their level and play their game. It was cool though, just as long as they let me go.

"We're gonna release you, but you have to leave... just like the smart folks are doing," the smart mouthed officer that was across from me shot sarcastically.

That shit rubbed me the wrong way, but I held my tongue as I watched the crowd disperse to their cars. "Well, can I go?" I repeated.

The cop holding me released my arm with a warning to leave. *I'm leaving, but not until I speak my peace to this bitch right here!*

Eyeing Tangi standing there chatting it up with some woman, my anger rose, and I began to stride swiftly in her direction. She lifted her head just as I made it into her personal space.

"Can you excuse us please?" I asked the lady Tangi was speaking to.

"No Tracy...you don't have to leave and Momma Armstrong, we don't have anything to say to each other!"

"You might not have shit to say to me, but I got a mouth load for your homewrecking ass!" I blurted out embarrassing her in front of her friend, who hurried up and ran off. Probably to go get some help, and that was a good thing because after I beat Tangi's ass she was going to need some fucking help!

"You need to crawl back under whatever lil rock you crawled from under because you haven't been around in years. And now, all of a sudden, Dallas is your main concern?"

"Bitch you ain't seen me because my son was obviously hiding your sneaky ass!" I hissed and rolled my eyes with my fists balled up.

"I'm not gonna stand here and entertain your bullshit!" Tangi snapped. "My mom always said to respect my elders and considering you old as shit..."

Before I swung, I checked the area for witnesses. Once I confirmed the coast was clear, I popped that bitch right in the eye. She didn't fall, but that ho' was hollering and so was I when I ran off laughing!

That's what she the fuck gets! All this is her fault for fucking a married man. If it wasn't my son, it would've been someone else's man! Tangi was a certified tramp in my eyes and if I found out she had something to do with Dallas being missing, a black eye would be the least of her worries.

Driving off from the scene, I made my way home. It was getting late and I was worn out. I had barely gotten any sleep since all the craziness had begun.

"Damn!" I groaned in pain as I gripped the steering wheel as I glanced down at my swollen knuckles.

Making it back to the house around midnight, I snatched my silky black wig off soon as I got inside. I put it on the Styrofoam head because I took care of my hair. That shit costs me a real pretty penny, so I couldn't afford to get them tangled. Then I went to the kitchen to get ice for my hand and a bottle of red wine for my nerves. They were wrecked and I definitely needed a drink.

"Here I am... all alone," I sighed heavily.

Feeling sorry for myself wasn't on the agenda. I had to sit there and force some positive thoughts into my head. There weren't many.

KNOCK! KNOCK! KNOCK!

"Who the hell is this at my door at this time of night?" I whispered as I got my gun out of my purse and removed the safety before creeping to the front.

Peeking out the window to the left, I drew the sheer white curtains back and saw two officers with trench coats on. They looked more like detectives.

As my heart raced, I prayed that they weren't here to deliver bad news. I took a deep breath and slowly opened the door. "Can I help you?"

The two detectives flashed their badges and introduced themselves before asking if they could come in. I obliged, but got right down to it. I needed to know what was going on.

"Did you find my son? Did you find Dallas?" I panicked with sweat dripping profusely from my armpits.

"We didn't find a body, but we found blood and DNA at a potential crime scene..."

"Are you saying that my son is dead?!" I screamed to the top of my lungs as the tears flowed heavily.

Dropping to my knees, I began to pray as the detectives tried to explain what they found. It didn't even matter what that was if it wasn't my son or the people responsible for his absence!

"Do you know who did it?"

"Well, since we don't know what was done to your son..."

"But you know something was done to him? I mean, my son didn't just up and disappear!" I cried as tears continued to rain down my cheeks.

"We just need to ask you a few questions. Are you up to answering them?"

"Look, I done told you everything I know and gave you a whole fucking list of suspects! Yet, here you are talking about blood and DNA! You don't have a body or a suspect so again, why are you here?!" I screamed becoming more upset by the second. "Oh, I know! You guys saw me making noise with the rally tonight and wanna act like y'all been investigating! Get the fuck outta here and go investigate the folks on that list I gave you! Do that and I guarantee you find the person responsible for my missing boy! Do that and I guarantee y'all lazy asses will win some brownie points with the community, since obviously that's all y'all care about!"

I had enough! They had to go, and I put their asses right on out too!

That night I went to bed with a headache and woke up with an even bigger one when my phone rang with somebody from the hospital asking me to come down and view a body. "Is it my son? Is it Dallas Armstrong?"

The woman on the phone couldn't tell me shit, but she did have me down there in record time. I didn't even take the time to brush my teeth. I just popped a piece of gum in my mouth and kept it moving all the way to the hospital, shaking and crying the entire ride.

Parking illegally, I ran inside to the information desk of the emergency department and gave them my name. The lady punched some information into the computer then directed me down the hall where the morgue was located.

My nerves were literally wrecked as I took the elevator down and exited into a cold dimly lit hallway leading to a glass enclosure where a woman sat. Traveling slowly to it, I tapped to get her attention.

"How may I help you?" After giving her my name and identification, she came around and escorted me to a window with a curtain. "I'm going to open this up and you tell me if you can identify the body. Take as much time as you need. Are you ready?"

As we stood there in silence, I inhaled and held my breath until the cold metal table holding a dead man appeared. "Ooooo!" I hollered out and dropped down to the floor.

"Ma'am, is this your son?"

I guess I was so riled up that I burst out in loud cries. Not because the body was not Dallas', but because he was still out there somewhere...

Running out of the hospital hysterically, I made it to my car and rushed back home. I needed a drink and a smoke. I even stopped by the store and bought a pack of Kool Filter Kings!

I hadn't smoked in years, but I had to in order to calm my nerves. Firing up the first one in the car, I choked so hard that I slightly peed on myself and had to pull over. It was all bad!

Taking my ass home, I showered and began drinking. The drunker I got, the more I thought about Tangi and her brother Jay and wondered if they were behind Dallas' disappearance.

A big brother is gonna ride or die for their baby sister! That shit right there is a fact!

I didn't know how much truth my suspicions held, but I sure as hell was going to follow up on them!

Chapter Seventeen

Smooth

I was cleaning up the kitchen when my eyes caught sight of some papers on Tangi's counter. Of course, being as curious as I was, I started to look through them. My mouth literally hit the floor when I saw what the contents of those papers were. I could've gone back to the bedroom to ask Tangi about them, but instead, I panicked and ran. I needed time to process her test results and calculate some shit. Once I did, I really felt stupid.

"Tangi is pregnant and that's my fucking baby she's carrying!" I whispered as I sat in my car still staring at the proof in my hands. I couldn't believe it.

Knowing that I couldn't run from it, I had to go back. I had to go talk to Tangi about it. I was sure she was wondering where I was anyway.

Driving back over to her house, I found her car gone and her lights off inside the house. I couldn't imagine where she could've gone at this time of night.

"Maybe she went to the hospital?" I thought out loud as I pulled the number up using Google.

After calling up there, I found out that she hadn't checked in. That had me confused and I was about to start tripping. But before I had the chance, Tangi pulled into the driveway.

Allowing her to park, I got out and greeted her before she made it to the door. When she turned to me, my face turned up.

"What the hell happened baby?" I asked filled with a mixture of concern and anger as I gazed at her black eye. "Who the fuck did this to you?"

"It's nothing Smooth!" she insisted as she unlocked the door and went inside.

Trailing behind her to the bedroom, I watched her flop onto the bed in frustration. "You wanna talk about that black eye?"

"No, because I told you that I'm fine!"

"Well, how about we talk about the baby?"

She huffed and looked at me. "I was going to tell you..."

"When?"

"To be honest, I was looking for the papers so I could give them to you when you came back to the bedroom, but then I remembered they were on the kitchen counter. When I went for them, you and the papers were gone!"

"I meant to have a discussion with you, but I needed a little time to think. I mean, it was just a shock, ya know?" I asked.

"Yea, I feel that?"

"Are you okay?"

"I'm fine. I actually feel better than I've felt in a long time. For some reason, this pregnancy feels different than the first time," she said.

"Well, maybe because we somehow found our way back to one another again. Look babe, I love you. I never stopped loving you. I was so worried about you when you had just up and disappeared. I thought about you every single day and practically begged Jay to give me your number or location... something. But shit, your brother is so damn stubborn. I know it's cuz he's protective of you though..."

"Yea, he's always been that way. He's the best big brother I could've asked for though."

"Yea. Enough about Jay though. Now that all your secrets are out, I just wanna know what you want. I mean, we're having a baby together. The baby is mine, right?"

"Of course, the baby is yours."

"So, what do you want? Do you wanna be with me or do you just want us to be co-parents? Me... I wanna be with you. I want us to get married so we can give our baby a secure family. I love you very much, so you gotta let me know what you wanna do."

I just wanted her to know that I was here for her. I wanted her to know that even if all she wanted was to co-parent our baby, I'd be there for her. Of course, I'd be a little hurt because I wanted much more than that from her. But I couldn't force her to be with me if that wasn't what she wanted.

"Ever since I found out that I was pregnant again, I was a little confused. I didn't know if you'd be happy or feel something else. I didn't know if you hated me or what your feelings were..."

"Hate you? Babe, I could never hate you," I said as I pulled her in my arms. "Since you've been gone, my love for you only grew. I want us to get married. I wanna give you my last name and I'd like to do that before the baby comes. What you think?" I asked.

"Wait... what?"

"You heard me. I love you and I wanna get married as soon as possible. We can fly to Vegas or get married at the courthouse downtown. Whatever you wanna do, I'm with it as long as we husband and wife at the end of the day," I stated.

"You're serious, aren't you?"

"I've never been more serious in my life. So, whaddya say?"

She pretended to be thinking long and hard, but finally, a huge smile graced her face. "I say let's get married!!" she said as she jumped in my arms and wrapped her legs around my waist.

As she planted her lips on mine and I drove my tongue deep inside her mouth. I had waited so long to kiss her like this. With Tangi still in my arms, I cradled her and took a few steps over to the bed. Gently placing her body on top of the thick purple comforter, I hovered over her and kissed her passionately.

That night was going to be a long night filled with great make up sex and good loving. It was something that was long overdue...

Chapter Eighteen

Tierra

One month later...

I was sitting down rocking Miracle to sleep when a 'BREAKING NEWS' segment interrupted my favorite soap opera. I didn't know what the hell they were reporting, but I was hoping that it was something about the little girl who had disappeared almost two weeks ago. Instead, it was news about a body being found in the Buffalo Bayou.

What the hell? Who would dump a body in the middle of a damn bayou? It wasn't as if the water was that deep. As the reporter spoke about the body, he said it was wrapped in blue tarp and taped with duct tape. It appeared the body had been attached to a couple of cinder blocks, but one of them got disconnected causing the body to float upward. The body was described as an African American male, but because of decomposition, no other description was given. He said the body had been in the water for so long the only way they'd be able to identify it was through dental records because of decomposition.

"Ugh! I could only imagine how that shit smells!"

Miracle turned in my arms as I continued to hum to her while trying to listen to the news. They said that more information would become available as soon as they were done with the testing. The Young & the Restless returned to the television, but my mind was already shot. What if that body was Dallas? The reporter did say it was an African American male. I picked up my phone and called Thaddeus.

"Hey baby, what's up?"

"Hey, they found a body," I blurted out.

"What body? What are you talking about?"

"I was watching my stories and they interrupted with breaking news. They found a body in Buffalo Bayou!"

"Okay, so?"

"It's an African American man!"

"Babe, what are you getting at?" he asked.

"I think it might be Dallas!"

"Babe, you watch too much MacGyver. That body could be anybody, but you think it might be Dallas..."

"Because he's the only black man I know that's missing!"

"Right. But just because he's the only dude you know that's missing doesn't mean he is the only dude missing. You're jumping to conclusions way too soon. If they just found the body, in the bayou at that, it probably means whoever it is all fucked up. They'll probably take weeks identifying that nigga because they gon' have to use his dental records."

"Yea, that's what the news said," I confirmed.

"Right. So, if I was you, I'd just calm down and go on about my business. I mean, so what if it is Dallas? After everything that sorry ass nigga put you through, I say good fuckin' riddance!" he exclaimed. "Now look, I gotta go. I have a client here and he's looking at me all crazy and shit. Love you."

"Okay, love you too."

I ended the call and went to put the baby in her crib. I couldn't believe that Thaddeus didn't care if Dallas was dead or alive. But then again, I couldn't understand why I cared. Dallas had done a ton of shit to me during the last year of our marriage. He also acted the damn fool once I filed for divorce. But we shared a little girl together, even though I wasn't allowing him to see her. Man, this shit had my emotions so conflicted.

On one hand, I didn't want him anywhere near our daughter. On the other hand, he was still her father. His blood ran through her veins just like mine. I always heard people say that children needed both of their parents. I was happy and lucky to have had both of mine in my life...my father passed away a few years ago. Dallas also had both of his parents in his life when he was growing up. I guess that's why he suddenly had a change of heart concerning our little girl because at first, he didn't care about her one bit.

If he had just stepped up from the beginning, we probably would've had a much better relationship even if we were divorced. But noooooo! He was too busy plotting to leave me so he could be with my best friend. I would never forgive him for that shit because I really loved him.

It would've been one thing if we had problems in our marriage, but we didn't. I worked and contributed to the bills. I cooked, cleaned and fucked him on the regular. What more had he needed to be happy with me?

I hadn't seen Tangi since that night at the rally. She wanted to act as though we were still besties, but how could we ever get that closeness back when I didn't trust her at all. Of course, I didn't hate her. She had been like a sister to me for years. It caused me a great deal of pain to not be in her life. It caused me an even bigger amount of pain to not have her involved in Miracle's life. She was supposed to be my little girl's godmother. We had made that promise to each other when we were younger.

Why did she have to betray me that way? I mean, hadn't I been a good friend to her? Hadn't I always been there when she needed me? What had I done that warranted her stabbing me in the back that way?

I decided to make a pot of coffee. No sense in giving myself a headache for nothing. These questions would never be answered because Tangi and I hadn't talked about them. While my coffee was brewing, my head kept spinning from unanswered questions.

KNOCK! KNOCK! KNOCK!

Thank God! I welcomed the distraction to take my mind off of all this shit. I walked over to the door praying it wasn't the police coming to question me again. I pulled the door back and there stood Tangi. I didn't know what the hell she wanted, but what I wanted was to bust her in the face. I still hadn't gotten payback for what she did to me, but instead of fucking her up, I decided now might be a good time to get some of those questions answered.

I crossed my arms over my chest and stared at her. "What do you want?"

When my eyes landed on her belly, I saw that she was pregnant. It was only a small bump, but it was noticeable, nonetheless.

"Can I come in?" she asked looking shy and timid.

I wanted to tell her, *Don't look shy now bitch! Where was all this shyness when you were fucking my husband?!* But I didn't do that. Instead, I stepped aside and allowed her to come in. I mean, the only way I'd get those answers was to sit with her and ask the questions, right?

"Would you like some coffee?" I asked.

"Sure."

She took a seat at the breakfast table while I made us each a cup of coffee. Mine with three scoops of cream and two sugars, hers with two scoops of cream and three sugars. It was funny the shit you remembered even though you and your bestie weren't speaking. I placed the cup on the table before her and sat down opposite her.

"What brings you here?" I asked as I took a sip of the hot liquid.

"I uh, I saw the news, so I thought I'd come by to make sure you were alright."

"I'm fine. Why wouldn't I be?"

"Well, the news said it was a black man in the bayou. I figured with Dallas being missing and all..."

"Dallas is no longer my concern. We're divorced and weren't even on good terms when he went missing," I stated.

"Yea, I know. Look Tierra, I owe you a huge apology..."

"Ya think?"

"I know what I did was wrong and fucked up..."

"Why?"

"Huh?"

"Why did you do it? We were like sisters! I shared everything with you! Why would you hurt me like that?" I asked. I had wanted to know why she had sex with my husband for a long ass time. I was finally going to get the answer.

"I don't know why..."

"Oh no, bitch! I waited too fuckin' long for an answer to that question. For you to say you don't know why ain't gonna cut it for me!" I said. "There had to be a reason why you fell in bed with my husband. I need you to tell me what that reason was."

"I really don't know Tierra. I never planned or meant for things to happen the way that they did. I never wanted to sleep with Dallas..."

"Shit, you must've wanted it because you opened your legs for the dick!" I said with a grimace.

"I was wrong Tierra. I crossed a line that should've never been crossed..."

"Ya gotdamn right! We were like sisters! Best friends above all else and you destroyed that! How could you have been so selfish Tangi? You introduced me to Dallas. Shit, if you wanted him, then you should've kept him!"

"I didn't want him. I don't know what happened or how things got out of hand..."

"Stop saying you don't know when you do know! Own yo' shit!"

"I am owning it Tierra!"

"No, you're not. You're sitting here talking about you don't know why you fucked him, but you have to know. If you don't know, who the fuck gonna know for you?" I asked.

I was pissed and tired of her trying to play the damn victim. She wasn't the victim...I was. I had put everything into our friendship because I loved Tangi. I just don't understand how she could do me like that. I would've never stooped so low. I would've never done anything like that to her. As a matter of fact, I would've done anything FOR her because that was how much I loved her.

"I've apologized to you Tierra. What more can I do or say to make you believe how sorry I am?" she asked with tears in her eyes.

"I just don't understand how you could've done me like that, or you thought that was okay."

"I knew it wasn't okay Tierra. I tried to stop messing with Dallas on more than one occasion, but he wouldn't leave me alone. He always managed to come back around, and I always fell for it. I never wanted or meant to hurt you. If I could take all that shit back, I would. None of that was worth the pain that I caused you."

"I would've never done that to you."

"I know. I hate that I ruined our friendship. I'm missing out on so much with you and Miracle. And I'm having my first baby too," she said as she patted her small round belly.

"I saw that. Congratulations," I said.

"Thank you."

See... that was another moment we were supposed to be sharing together. However, she had ruined it.

Damn, I just wish that shit could go back to the way they used to be. But I knew better. Things would never be the same with us again...

Chapter Nineteen

Tangi

I don't know what possessed me to come over to Tierra's place. Hell, I knew shit wasn't going to magically be okay between us. It's just that when I saw the news about the body being found in the bayou, the first person I thought of was her. I figured that if it was Dallas, she'd need some support. That's why I came. I wanted to support her, but in order for me to do that, I had to apologize again. I just wanted her to accept it so we could move on, but of course, that was only in a perfect world.

Now that I was pregnant, I wanted my best friend back. I needed her now more than ever before. I was getting married in a few weeks and I wanted her by my side, but if we couldn't get past this wall between us, I knew that wasn't going to happen. She had every right to be upset with me. I had betrayed her in the worst way. I understood the anger she felt toward me. Hell, I was her closest friend and I had screwed her over.

"Tierra, what's it going to take for us to get our friendship back on track?" I asked.

She scoffed at me for a second as if I had just asked if we could have sex. "I don't know if we will ever get this friendship back on track. To be honest, I can't trust you. I don't know if I'll ever be able to trust you again," she responded.

"But I'm having a baby," I said with tears in my eyes.

"Right, and I have a baby."

"I just think back to the promises we made about being each other's baby's godmothers. I still want you to be my baby's godmother, even if you don't want me to be yours..."

"I don't know if I can do that..."

"Why not?"

"Because being the godmother to your baby will require a certain amount of closeness between us. We aren't even on that level. We're barely on speaking terms," she admitted.

"That's true, but there's no one I trust to be my baby's godmother more than you."

"I wish I could say the same about you," she replied sadly.

"I wish I could turn back the hands of time and take back everything I did to hurt you, but I can't. All I want now is for us to move past it so we can be friends again," I said.

"That's what you're not getting. I don't know if we can ever repair this broken friendship. I can't even look at you without thinking about what you and Dallas did. Like, I was confiding in you about my husband's infidelities. I asked you to help me find the woman who he was cheating on me with. You know what you said?"

"Tierra…"

"No, no! Do you remember what you said to me…what advice you offered as my best friend? You told me to let it go and forget about it. You said if I wanted to save my marriage, I needed to forget about the other woman and move on! Great advice considering you were the other woman!!" she fumed.

That shit there made my heart and head hurt. She was right. I had said those things to her because I didn't want her to find out that the bitch she was talking about was me.

"I'm so sorry!"

"Yea, you're sorry now because you got caught! If I wouldn't have overheard your conversation that night, were you ever going to tell me or were you just going to keep playing me for a fool?"

"I was wrong on so many levels, but all I can do now is apologize. There's nothing else I can say or do except say I'm sorry. Don't you think I hate myself for what I did to you? You were my best friend in the whole world!

I was bogus as fuck for what I did, but I can't change it. I can never go back and change what I did...no matter how badly I want to," I said as the tears welled up in my eyes again.

Looking at the pain in Tierra's eyes made me feel ten times worse than I already felt, I loved Tierra, but what I had done was over. I wasn't seeing Dallas anymore. I was engaged to a wonderful man, who was also the father of my unborn baby.

"I'm getting married in Vegas in a few weeks. I was hoping that you would stand up for me..." I stopped talking because of the way she was looking at me. She was staring at me as if to say she couldn't understand how I had the audacity to ask that of her. "Maybe it was a mistake to come here. Just know that I love you Tierra. I hope that one day you will find it in your heart to forgive me."

I stood up and made my way toward the door. There wasn't anything left for me to say. She obviously wasn't trying to hear shit that I had to say and wasn't ready to forgive me. I couldn't blame her though because had the shoe been on the other foot, a bitch wouldn't have even made it inside my house let alone had a cup of coffee. That just goes to show that she has a bigger heart than I did.

Chapter Twenty

Smooth

For the past month Tangi and I had been spending time together nearly every day bringing us even closer. We hadn't moved in together yet, but I did have a key to her place. The only reason why we weren't shacking up already was because Tangi wanted to wait until after the wedding.

Respecting her wishes, I fell back on that issue and focused on making her as happy as I could while she was carrying my baby. Just like she was when we first got back together, she couldn't stop smiling if I paid her ass to. But lately, she had been nothing but sad eyes and tears.

At first, I blamed it on her crazy hormones, but when she started complaining about not having Tierra around her to help her with certain things I knew exactly what it was. Now I needed to find out a way to fix their friendship, or at least get them on cordial terms until their wounds could mend. Learning to trust would take some time, but I had to begin somewhere.

"I'm out man!" Throwing my hand in the air, I left the club and went to Tangi's so that I could talk to her about the wedding. She didn't have a matron of honor yet and that wasn't sitting well with her. It was actually throwing our vibe off every time we discussed it.

The ride over there, all I could think about was giving Tangi the perfect ceremony. Not because that was what she deserved after the trouble she helped create, but because I was in love with her and she was having my kid. That shit right there was enough to lock Tangi down just like I was about to do.

Entering into her house 40 minutes later using my key, I found Tangi in her room on the floor in a fetal position crying her eyes out. "What happened? Are you aight? Is it the baby?" I panicked as I bent down and held on to her.

"She hates me! No matter how truthful I am, it always backfires, and I end up getting disliked even more! Fuck it! I'll just be friendless for the rest of my life because I'm never gonna find anybody like Tierra! Why did I have to do that dumb shit and why do I have to pay for it for the rest of my life?! I'm sorry! I'm sorry to you, I'm sorry to her... I'm sorry to everyone for everything I've ever done!" she screamed snatching from me then running to the bathroom to lock herself in.

"Wow!" I sighed not realizing how much the shit was bothering Tangi. Sure, I could've told her to shake it off and keep moving, but then I would've hurt her feelings. Damn! I didn't know what to do.

Reaching out to Jay while Tangi was in the bathroom, I got him on the phone and told him what his sister was going through. Concern filled his voice when he asked where she was and if she was okay.

"Nah, the only way she's gonna come out of this shit is if we go straight to Tierra and talk to her," I suggested.

"Nigga bye!" Jay clowned. "That girl ain't gonna listen to us! She done already made it clear that we're the fuckin' enemies..."

"Nah, let's go over there with some gifts for the baby and just talk to her. If that don't work, at least I know we tried." I sighed heavily while running my hand down my face as I switched the phone from my left ear to my right. "I just really wanted your sister to have the perfect wedding and this is the only way I see that shit happening."

"Damn, you do love Tangi, huh?" Jay teased loudly.

"Hell yeah, nigga! What you thought it was a game?!" I clowned as I listened to the bathroom doorknob rattling.

"Nigga meet me back down at the club and we'll go over to Tierra's. If you could convince me to do this high school shit, then I know you have a shot of making Tierra listen to you!" Jay laughed before hanging up.

Looking over at Tangi, I smiled and went and held her. "Baby, get some rest and I'll have a surprise for you when you wake up."

Yeah, I promised my baby that shit, and I planned on making good on that promise too! Now it may not be getting Tierra to forgive her, but I wasn't about to come home empty handed either!

Contemplating a backup plan as I drove back to the club, I kept coming up empty. The only thing I could think of was getting her a wedding gift, something shiny with a lot of carats.

Still clueless to what I was going to bring Tangi when I returned, I pulled up in the lot and saw Jay sitting inside his ride while it quietly idled. Parking my car beside his, I got out, hit the locks and hopped in the car with my boy.

"I hope you got a plan Smooth, because that shit sounded really good on the phone. Now that my high done came down, this sounds like some foolish ass shit nigga!"

Waving my hand at him to shoo off his ridiculous remarks, I instructed him to the mall. When we got there, we both went in and spent about a grand a piece on just a few unique items then we were off to Tierra's.

On the short drive, I went over and over what I was going to say to Tierra. Thing is, when we got there and parked, all that shit I silently rehearsed went flying out the window.

"You need me to come with you?" Jay laughed as he got comfortable in his seat like he had no plans to get his ass out once we spotted Tierra outside fiddling in the yard.

"Nigga, if you don't get out this damn ride and help me!" I grunted and mean mugged him as I opened my door. "Two folks pleading the case is always better than one!"

"Ain't nobody about to beg that bitch for shit!" Jay hissed as Tierra approached the car. "At least not this nigga!"

"This is for your sister! Remember that," I said.

"Hey guys! What brings you two over here?" Tierra asked as she eyed us suspiciously.

"We came to bring you these gifts for the baby." I said quickly thinking as I urged Jay to get the hell out and grab something.

That nigga got the hint and started helping me out. "Yeah, with all this crazy shit going on, I haven't had a chance to get the baby anything. Then, with all the shit with you and sis... I didn't know if you were mad at me too," Jay said all smiles and shit. Tierra was falling for that shit too. It was like she had a change of heart.

"No! I'm not trippin' Jay! Thanks both you guys! You really didn't have to do all this! Miracle is spoiled rotten already!" She screamed happily as she squeezed the big stuffed gold lion with the purple ribbon. "This will go great with the theme of her room!"

"Cool, so, I guess we won't hold you up..." Jay said making me interrupt him. We didn't come all the way over there just to take some damn gifts! I needed Tierra and Tangi to make up!

"Nah, wait..." I said gaining Tierra's attention.

"Yeah, what's up?"

"I know I ain't got no business putting my nose up in you and Tangi's shit, but I love her and I want to see her happy despite all her wrongdoings." I said losing eye contact just long enough to glance over at Jay who was now leaning against his car with his arms folded. "I'm not gonna stand here and beg you to forgive her. I know all about what she did, and I understand why you're upset. I just wanna let you know how torn up she's been over the past few months behind all this. She misses you and..."

"And she wants you to be there at her wedding and she wants to be in the baby's life. Bottom line, she just wants her friend back!" Jay interrupted with his hands thrown up. "You over here getting all sentimental and shit...ain't nobody got time for that shit!"

"No! I think it's sweet how he's pleading a good case for Tangi! I'm a lil impressed!" Tierra laughed and as she stepped backwards, her vision suddenly shot to something behind us. Both Jay and I turned around to see a car coming full speed ahead.

"I know this bitch ain't coming back to my house!" Tierra screamed as Dallas' mother brought her vehicle to a screeching halt beside us before leaping out. The look on her face already told me what was about to go down and it wasn't going to be good.

"Ah, hah!" she hollered taking turns shaking her long fat finger at each of us. "I caught you guys all together plotting and trying to cover up your tracks, huh?! All you guys are in this shit together and I'm gonna prove it!"

"No! Let me prove something to you!" Tierra hollered back as she dug in the back of her waist and came out with a small chrome revolver. "Take one step on my property and I'm gonna prove to you that I'm done playing with your ass! I refuse to allow you to torment and terrorize me the way your son had been doing before his ass disappeared! Now you got two minutes to get the fuck outta here on your own. If not, I can help you by calling the police, the ambulance or the coroner! I'm gonna let the choice be yours!"

"Bitch the law is already on the way! Go ahead on and wave that lil granny pea shooter if you want to! This time I brought some back up!" Dallas' mother clowned and reared back from Tierra's property line.

In the midst of all the arguing, two more cars came flying up. This time they were police vehicles. Tierra had tucked her gun away when she saw the cruisers heading our way.

Four cops got out, but only one spoke. The short stubby white guy with the potbelly eased forward and tried to calm us all down.

"I'm glad you're all here!" he belted out as he went down a list that he was holding in his grip. "We have some new findings and we need some answers! Until we get them, all of you are suspects and one more young lady as well... ah, Tangi..."

"What the hell she gotta do with it?" I snapped looking at everyone. Jay shrugged and so did Tierra.

"Ain't she the side chick?! The side chick is always a suspect!" Dallas' mother spoke out rudely.

"And so is the mother!" another cop added as he joined us while the other two hung back. "We followed leads from the crime scene and forensics proved you were there. We also have evidence of you firing your weapon. Do you have that weapon with you right now Ms. Armstrong?!"

"What?!" Dallas' mother screamed hysterically. "Are you saying it was my boy y'all found in the bayou, huh? Was it my boy?"

"Ma'am, I'm sorry. Yes, it was your son's body we recovered in the bayou. I'm sorry for your loss," one of the cops said.

Instead of Ms. Armstrong throwing herself to the ground in a fit, she started trying to fight all of us. She was trying to get all of us locked up!

All this shit because that nigga Dallas got obsessed with his wife's best friend. This shit don't make no damn sense...

Chapter Twenty-One

Ms. Armstrong

"I wanna see my boy!" I told the cops once they had slapped the cuffs on my ass to get me to calm down.

"I don't think that's a good idea ma'am."

"I wanna see my son!"

"Your son's body was submerged in the water for weeks according to the medical examiner. That's why we had to identify him with dental records. You won't be able to recognize him," the cop stated.

"Oh My God!" I cried. Tears were raining from my eyes at what they told me. I didn't care about all that though. I had to see my son.

I was his mother, and no one knew him the way that I did. It didn't matter what condition his body was in. He was still my son and I loved him unconditionally. That meant that he could look like a sack of shit and I'd still love him because he was my boy.

"I WANT TO SEE MY SON!!" I yelled.

"If she wants to see him, I say we let her," one of the cops said with a smile on his face.

"Okay ma'am."

They helped me into the rear of their cruiser because at that point, I was in no condition to drive. My son had been sitting at the bottom of some bayou all this time while we were out there looking for him. All this time he was in that old dirty, muddy water.

"Why? Why didn't you arrest any of them? I just know one of them killed my son!" Not one of those bastards offered me any comfort when they heard my son was dead. Tierra was once married to my son and didn't even ask if she could drive me to the hospital. I had to be driven there with these cops and deal with that by myself.

"Why didn't you arrest those bastards? I know one of them killed my son!!"

My cries landed on deaf ears once again. Neither the cop driving nor the one sitting beside him listened or responded to shit I was saying. The only one that I knew would was the Lord above. So, to him I prayed...

"I don't know who ended my son's life, but please let them pay. Let the truth come out..."

Right in the middle of my chanting, the officer driving drowned me out with the police radio. I just yelled over that shit and showed them they couldn't stop my conversation with the Lord.

"Make these fools pay..." I continued before the car came to an abrupt stop slinging my body forward so hard that my forehead went crashing into the back of the seat.

Straightening out my shoulder length burgundy curly wig, I got out and went into the hospital like I did before, only this time the sight before me was surreal. The lady was wearing a face mask as if my son's body reeked.

"No! Not my boy! Not my son! Noooooooo!" I hollered and flipped out all over again. This time, the medics came to sedate me while a couple of nurses wheeled me off.

Waking up in the sterile hospital room a little while later, I felt woozy and sick to my stomach realizing that Dallas was truly dead. That was a mother's worst nightmare, to outlive their children. It was an indescribable heartache that could only begin to heal after the folks in charge of his death paid dearly. I wouldn't rest until that happened.

As I sat in the hospital bed and cried, a nurse walked in asking how I was feeling. "How do you think I feel? I just saw my son's dead body and he looked like a creature from the fuckin' swamp!"

"I'm sorry for your loss ma'am," she said.

"Whatever! When the hell can I get out of here?" I asked.

"Let me get the doctor." She hurriedly left the room to go get the doctor.

She returned a short time later with a doctor. "How are you feeling Ms. Armstrong? I mean, I heard about your son and I'm so deeply sorry for your loss. Is there someone who can come and pick you up so you won't be alone?"

"Look doc, I appreciate your concern, but I'll be fine. I just need to get out of here because I gotta plan for my son's funeral," I said. "I mean, I can go right?"

"Yes ma'am. You were just brought here to rest because of everything you've been through. I'll get your release papers signed." He and the nurse left the room and the nurse returned alone about ten minutes later. She handed me the paperwork and looked at me sadly.

"Again, I'm sorry about your son."

"Thanks!" I said as I walked out of the room.

I was heading for the door when I remembered I didn't have a ride. "Wait! What happened to my car!?" I mumbled to myself.

"Ms. Armstrong!" the guard called out to me as I stood there in confusion. Then I remembered that I had left my fucking car near Tierra's house. Shit! The man walked over to me and handed me a business card. "The cops left this information for you."

"What's this?"

"That's where they towed your car to ma'am," he stated before walking off. I couldn't believe that shit. After everything that I had been through, now I had to hunt down my damn car.

Things seemed to go from terrible to horrific. It was too much, and I couldn't handle it. I had to go home.

I had never used my Uber app before, even though Dallas had installed it over a year ago. I smiled and looked up above and thanked him. Then I had a thought.

I sure hope he made it to heaven...

Lost in my thoughts, I traveled home in a blur. Nothing made sense anymore. The only thing that did was revenge. I had to have it.

"If I gotta kill those bastards one by one, then that's what I gotta do! Somebody has to pay for this shit!"

Dallas was my only child, so what was I going to do without him. My husband was already gone. I mean, what the hell did I have left to lose?

Without thinking, I got in my truck that I rarely drove and headed back out to Tierra's house. She acted so calm and collected when the cops announced that Dallas was dead. Nobody acted out but me. That shit right there meant that I was the only one that cared.

"I'm gonna go over there and put this shit on her ass! I'm gonna fill her body up until it stops moving! I fucking hate her for not caring about Dallas! I didn't care if my son fucked a million other bitches on her ass, she had no right to disregard his life like he meant nothing! I mean, how could she?! She had his only child!"

Not giving a damn about the consequences, I drove up to the end of Tierra's block and parked. I wasn't mad enough to go take her life, so I had to talk myself into it and ask for forgiveness all at once. It was a very difficult task.

As I sat there contemplating my next move, I saw Tierra's man pull up. When he parked and got out, I watched as my ex daughter-in-law came out to greet him with a kiss.

How the fuck was this bitch so happy after she just found out that Dallas was dead?! No! That shit wasn't sitting well at all!

Boldly getting out of my car, I cocked my gun and got as close as I could before ducking behind a parked car and letting loose. My aim was all over the place, but I didn't stop blasting until my clip was empty. I knew I had hit a window because I heard the glass break. I think I hit a tree, but couldn't be sure. The only thing I was sure of was that I had put at least one round in Tierra's man. Shit, she was the one I really wanted to shoot, and I didn't even graze the bitch. But I did see her dude was bleeding from the chest.

As Tierra began screaming like a damn fool, folks began to come out of their homes. I casually stuffed my gun in my skirt and walked calmly back to my car. Keying the ignition, I drove off slowly, making sure not to attract attention.

What had I done? I didn't even kill the main person I went over there to kill?!

"It's okay!" I chanted as I pulled over a few miles down the street and popped a new clip into my gun. "Tangi, I'm coming for you, your brother and your man next! I'll just have to go back for Tierra's ass!"

Going down to the club, I searched for any enemy I could find. It was still a little early so I had to sit across the street and wait.

Starting to feel restless after ten minutes of waiting, I went down the road to the liquor store and bought a fifth of Jack Daniels. It used to be Dallas' father's favorite.

Clinging on to the whiskey, I got back in the truck, drove back to my original spot and cracked open the alcohol bottle. I didn't need a glass. I did it the old school way and drank that shit straight from the bottle with no chaser.

"Where the fuck are they?!" I slurred as I began talking to myself. I knew I was fucked up when I started answering too. Shit, by then, I barely knew where I was!

The only thing that helped sober me up just a smidgen was when I spotted the car that Tangi's brother and man were in earlier at Tierra's. Shit, at least it looked like the car. I couldn't be too damn sure because I was a lil tipsy.

Getting out of the truck stumbling, I crossed the street and started yelling. "You muthafuckas killed my son!"

Squeezing the trigger, I began tapping it as I directed it towards the two dirty bastards. They were ducking and dodging everything I shot their way.

"You can't hide!" I yelled stepping closer before freezing in my tracks as the sirens approached.

My ass took off to the truck, still shooting until I emptied that second clip. It wasn't long before bullets came flying back my way. What the fuck? You mean to tell me these muthafuckas was trying to kill me...knowing that I was a grieving mother. I had no time to put another clip in. I had to get out of there fast.

I heard sirens as I made it to my vehicle, but before I could climb in, I felt a burning sensation from my back to my chest. I tried to get in the truck, but my fingers weren't gripping at the driver's side door the way I wanted to. I looked at my chest and saw red from the streetlight overhead. As the police cars and paramedics pulled in across the street, I slid down to the ground.

I wanted to scream for help, but nothing would come out. My breathing was already pretty shallow, and my chest burned. I tried to breathe, but I couldn't. I couldn't breathe, speak, see... nothing. I did hear footsteps growing nearer, but it was already too late.

I mean, I didn't wanna live anyway. What did I have to live for besides a lifetime in jail? My son and husband were probably waiting for me. I knew my son was in heaven... he was a good man. If he could see how Dallas and I had been acting I knew he wouldn't be happy. He was most likely turning in his grave right now.

I couldn't believe my life was ending this way. Shit, I had lived a good life though. I just hoped whoever buried my ass used one of my Beyoncé wigs. Lord knew how much I loved those wigs and since I was going to be laid to rest in my FINAL resting place, I wanted to look my best.

As my spit leaked outside of my mouth and I went into cardiac arrest, I thought, *I may not have gotten to kill the people involved, but I was sure that I made enough noise to keep his murder case open.*

I got one last prayer out before I took my last breath.
Please Lord, don't let my death be in vein...

Chapter Twenty-Two

Tierra

One minute I was greeting Thaddeus with a kiss and the next I was holding his bloody body in my arms. I couldn't believe it! First Dallas and now him!

As I quickly dialed 9-1-1 and got someone on the line, I rocked Thaddeus, who was unconscious and bleeding from the chest. Although he was still breathing, I was scared to death.

"Please! Please come now!"

"Help is on the way ma'am!" the emergency operator assured as she held me on the line. "Do you know if the assailant is still on the property?"

"No, but the shooting has stopped. I don't even know who would do something like this! The only ones I see outside now are my neighbors! Please send someone quick!" I cried.

Suddenly, I heard Miracle begin to holler from inside the house. "Oh God, my baby!!"

Hell, I hadn't even checked on the baby even though one of the windows had been broken by a bullet, I had to get to her and make sure she was alright. I gently laid Thaddeus' down and ran inside to get my baby girl. I gently picked her up and quickly checked her out before cradling her in my arms and shushing her.

Once she had quieted down and I was sure she was alright, I placed her in the stroller and strapped her down. I kissed her lightly on the forehead, stuck her pacifier in her mouth and parked her just inside the side door that led outside.

Rushing back out, I met the medics. They were already working on Thaddeus as they lifted him on the gurney and wheeled him into the ambulance. The police came next. Instead of assisting, they tried to pull me to the side and stop me from riding with my fiancé.

"We need to ask you a few questions..."

"Ask me at the hospital because I gotta go!" I insisted shaking away and taking off to get in the back of the ambulance. "Shit! Shit! Shit! Where are you taking him?"

"Houston Methodist!"

I had almost forgotten about my baby. I ran back toward the house and got my baby and purse, then locked the door.

I was going back to the rear of the ambulance, but they started backing out of the driveway. I quickly strapped Miracle in and climbed in the driver's seat. On the ride to the hospital, I called Tangi. I didn't know who else to call during a time like this.

She picked up right away. Good thing Jay had given me her number earlier. "Hello," she answered a little uncertainty in her voice.

"Tangi!" I called out as I cried.

"Tierra?! Oh my God! What's wrong?" she asked, concern etched in her voice.

"Tangi, Thaddeus was shot!"

"Oh my God! Where are you?" she hollered.

"Following the ambulance to the hospital!"

"Which hospital are y'all headed to?"

"Houston Methodist..."

"I'm on my way!"

"Can you please call my mom?"

"Of course. Text me the number and please... just try to remain positive. We'll be there soon," she promised.

"Thank you Tangi," I cried.

"No thanks needed sis. I'll be there soon."

We ended the call as I continued to follow the ambulance to the hospital. I was so nervous. When I saw the helicopter land and the ambulance pull into the parking lot, I immediately panicked. What is happening? Why is the helicopter here? I watched as the medics quickly pulled Thaddeus from the rear of the ambulance and rush over to the helicopter. I jumped out of the truck and approached them once they returned to the ambulance.

"What's going on?" I asked.

"Your husband stopped breathing, so we gave him CPR, but had to get the helicopter because it can get him to the hospital faster!" he explained.

"Is he gonna die?" I asked in a panic.

"Just get to the hospital ma'am."

I ran back to the truck and climbed in then took off to the hospital now in a bigger panic than before. I was scared to death that I was going to lose Thaddeus. How the hell could this have happened? Who the hell could've shot at us and why? We never did anything to anybody.

I cried and prayed the entire ride to the hospital. By the time I got there, my mom was already there. I knew she would get there first because she lived closer. As soon as I walked into the emergency room, my mom rushed over to me.

"Any word yet?" I asked her.

"They wouldn't give me any information. Here, give me the baby and maybe you can go find out what his condition is," my mom said.

I handed Miracle to her and rushed over to the nurses' station. "My name is Tierra Armstrong. My fiancé was brought in with a gunshot wound to the chest!"

"What's his name?"

"Thaddeus Wiltz!"

She typed in the information in the computer and looked up at me. "He's still in surgery. As soon as the doctors are done, they will come out and speak with you," she said.

"Thank you," I said.

As I turned to walk away, Tangi and Smooth came rushing through the emergency room doors. She immediately took me in her arms and held me tight. I was so happy that she was here. I knew her being here now wouldn't fix everything that happened with our relationship, but it was a start. I was grateful that she was here for me. It seemed as if she dropped everything just for me, and I was really appreciative of that.

"Any word yet on his condition?" she asked.

"No, I just asked, and she said that he was in surgery."

"Oh my God!"

"What happened?" Smooth asked.

"I don't know. Thaddeus had just pulled up, so I went outside to great him. All of a sudden, bullets started flying and stuff. And when I looked, Thaddeus was hit. The bullet hit him in the back and went through to his chest! What if he doesn't make it?" I cried.

"You can't think like that," Smooth said. "That's a big dude yea! I'm sure he's gonna be fine."

Smooth managed to get a semi smile out of me, but it couldn't take away my anxiety. We walked over to where my mom was sitting and holding the baby. I sat next to her as Tangi took the baby. My mom wrapped her arm around my shoulder and pulled me close.

"He's gonna be alright honey. You just have to keep the faith," she said.

"How about we say a prayer for Thaddeus?" Smooth suggested.

My mom and I nodded our heads and smiled. We all stood up and held hands as Smooth said a prayer.

"Lord we come to you today to ask that you heal Thaddeus. We ask that you cover him in your blood and keep him safe. He has a beautiful family waiting right here for him, so please help him get through this. In Jesus name we pray, Amen."

"Oh damn! I forgot to call Hakim!" I said as I pulled my phone out.

Stepping to the side, I dialed his number. He answered on the first ring. When I told him what happened, he immediately sounded distraught. He told me that he'd gather the family and meet us at the hospital. Half an hour later, the doctor came through the double doors.

"I'm looking for the family of Thaddeus Wiltz!"

We rushed up to him. "I'm his fiancée. How is he doctor?" I asked.

"Well, I was able to remove the bullet, but he's lost a lot of blood, so we had to give him two pints. That's the good news..."

"What's the bad news?" I asked as my body began to shake.

"The bad news is that he's in a coma."

"Oh my God! A coma?"

"Yes ma'am. The next 24 to 48 hours are critical, so he's in the intensive care unit. Once he stabilizes, we'll have him transferred to a more private room."

Hakim picked that moment to rush in. "Can we see him?" I asked.

"How's Thaddeus?" Hakim asked.

"He's in a coma but they got the bullet out," Smooth answered.

"Can we see him?" Hakim and I asked at the same time.

"I think the best thing for you all to do is go home and come back in the morning..."

"I'm not leaving until I see my brother!" Hakim insisted.

"I'm sorry sir, but your brother is in ICU and visiting hours are over," the doctor said.

"I need to make sure my brother is okay!" Hakim demanded.

"I'm sorry sir. It's out of my hands right now. Why don't you all get some rest and come back in the morning?"

"He's right. There's nothing you guys can do here. Why don't you all get some rest tonight? We can come back early in the morning. If something happens, the hospital has your numbers, right?" my mom asked.

"Well, I don't know since they didn't call me," Hakim smirked.

"I'm sorry for not calling sooner Hakim. Everything just happened so fast..."

"It's okay. I'm just gonna need you to tell me what exactly happened to my brother," he said.

So, as I explained what happened, my mom took the baby and headed to my place. Miracle was tired, cranky and hungry. Thank God my mom was here. Once I finished telling Hakim the story, we all stepped outside of the hospital.

Hakim got in his truck and left the parking lot in a huff. I think he was still salty about not being called as soon as the shooting happened. That was definitely my fault, but I wasn't thinking at the time. Surely, he could cut me some slack on that.

"Do you need us to go home with you?" Tangi asked.

"No, I think I've taken up enough of your time for the night," I said.

"Nonsense. If you need me, I'm there."

"Thanks, but mom's at home, so I think I'll be fine."

"Okay, but I'll meet you at your house in the morning and ride with you to the hospital, so your mom can stay with Miracle," Tangi offered.

"Thank you so much," I said as I fell into her arms.

"I love you Tierra. There ain't nothing I wouldn't do for you."

"I know that now, and I thank you."

"Uhm, I didn't want to tell you anymore bad news, but Momma Armstrong was killed earlier," Tangi said.

"What?! How? What happened?"

"Apparently, she went to the club and started shooting at Jay and Smooth," she said.

"Yea, that ol' lady came up over there screaming about the two of us killing her son. Like, she was literally trying to take us out..."

"What happened to her?"

"Shit, Jay shot back and got her ass!" Smooth said. "I mean, I sympathized with her about her son, but we weren't about to let her just shoot us like that."

"Wow! You don't think that she could've been the one shooting at y'all too?" Tangi asked.

"Noooo!" I said just a little too quickly. I mean, now that I thought about it, she was acting pretty irrational last time I saw her. She could've tried to kill me, and Thaddeus was just caught in the crossfire.

"Are you sure?" Tangi asked.

"Well, at first I didn't think so, but now... I mean, who else would be trying to kill me? I don't have any enemies, especially not with Dallas dead. Oh my God!" I cried as I burst into tears.

"What?" Tangi asked as she wrapped her arm around my shoulder.

"I'm the reason that Thaddeus is fighting for his life. I'm the reason that he might not make it," I cried on Tangi's shoulder.

"Hey, hey. The doctor never said anything about him not making it. He said once he stabilizes they'll move him to a private room. He's gonna be fine," Tangi assured.

I held on to her and Smooth real tight as I continued to cry. In that moment, I was so happy to have her here. I loved her so much and I don't know what I would've done without her.

She was definitely needed!

After about 20 minutes, I finally calmed down enough for us to go home. On the ride home, I prayed hard that Thaddeus would be okay. I don't know what I would do without him. I loved him so much. He had treated me like a queen ever since the first day we met.

All I wanted was for him to pull through so we could live happily ever after. *Now look!*

I couldn't believe Dallas' mom. How could she do that? Shit, she'd better be glad she was dead because if she wasn't, I would've probably killed her ass. Like how she gon' blame people for Dallas' death? Yea, somebody had killed him, but that didn't mean it was any of us. Dallas had done a lot of shit to a lot of people. The nerve of her to accuse us.

I hoped the two of them rotted in hell together...

Epilogue

Six months later...

Tangi

This past year had been one for the books baby. I mean, a real rollercoaster ride. Things had worked out for the best though. My friendship with Tierra was finally in a better place. We weren't at 100 percent yet, but I hoped we would be one day. She had leaned on me a lot while Thaddeus was in the hospital recovering. Thank God that he was released and would make a full recovery once he completed his physical therapy. I was glad that she chose to depend on me though because that's what helped our relationship progress. She saw how much I really loved her during that time.

I gave birth to my little boy a couple of weeks ago and we named him Samuel after his daddy. I was happy that Smooth allowed me to give our baby his name. He said it made him proud and even shed a tear when he signed the birth certificate. That was why I loved him so much.

Smooth had always been there for me when it counted, just like my brother Jay. Between the two of them, I felt very protected. Tierra and I were in such a great place that she finally allowed me to be Miracle's godmother, and she was Samuel's godmother. Things worked out better than I ever could've hoped.

Dallas' murder still remains unsolved. The fact that his body had been sitting in that bayou for so long caused evidence to deteriorate. Because of that, the police had nothing to go on when searching for the killer, especially since there was little to no evidence found at his place. I don't know who killed Dallas. He had made my life a living hell this past year, so to be honest, I was glad he wasn't around anymore. I was glad that he wouldn't be able to hurt another woman again.

I was also glad that everything was going well in my life. Sure, that little first baby secret still haunted me at times and made me feel just a little guilty, but not guilty enough to confess. I'd be damn if I'd ever put myself in a position to lose my man again. That baby I got rid of was for the best because it was Dallas' little seed.

Even though I have a little guilt, I have no regrets. I had decided that I'd take that shit with me to the grave because things were finally working in my favor.

As a matter of fact, things couldn't be better...

Tierra

Wow! All I can say is that I'm blessed.

Blessed because I got my man, my best friend, and my baby girl. I never would've imagined that Tangi and I would've found our way back to each other, but we did.

It took a tragedy to get us to a place we once knew... happiness. Tangi helped me when I needed her the most, just the same way she had always done. She had always been there for me, and I for her. Now that she had a child and I had a child we were closer than ever.

I never thought she and I would have made up but thank God we did. With Dallas out of the picture completely, we never spoke about him or what happened between the two of them. She apologized, I accepted, and we moved on.

Thaddeus recovered from his injuries and I was grateful. I don't know what I would've done if he had died that day. I needed him to be a father to our daughter. Yes, Miracle was biologically Dallas' child, but he wasn't here, and Thaddeus was. My daughter was his child in every sense of the word. He was a wonderful man to me and a fantastic daddy to my baby.

As for all the drama that unfolded that night, six months ago, evidence did show that Dallas' mom was the one who shot at us. I still couldn't believe she would had done some shit like that. I mean, what the hell did I ever do to her to deserve that? But hey, her son was a damn fool and now I knew why. The apple didn't fall far from the tree. Wherever the two of them were, be it hell or purgatory cuz I know they weren't lucky enough to get to heaven, I hoped they could see how happy Tangi and I were with our lives. Dallas had tried to break us, but he failed.

Our friendship was now on its way to being stronger than ever, and I couldn't be happier.

Smooth

I kissed my woman goodbye and headed to the club to meet up with Jay. Things between me and Tangi had been going better than I could have ever expected. We were getting married and she had given birth to my son. I was on top of the world. I was extremely happy that she and Tierra were able to make up because that had a lot to do with her happiness these days. Lord knows that things could've ended a totally different way if Dallas' mom had her way. Thank God, Jay's aim was a lot better than hers was.

That lil bitch was trying to take us all out because she thought we had killed her son. Hell, I bet y'all wondering who killed that nigga Dallas huh? Well, Tierra and Tangi had nothing to do with it and neither did Thaddeus who almost died behind that shit.

My thoughts went out the window as I walked in the club and locked the door because it wasn't open yet. I made my way to the back office where Jay was waiting for me.

"Wassup bro," he greeted as he gave me a brotherly hug.

"Nothing much. What's good?"

"Shit, everything good, ya heard me?"

We both laughed because he was right... everything was good. As a matter of fact, everything was great!

"Yea, I hear ya. Man, thank God things worked out the way that they did. Shit could've turned out a totally different way if we hadn't done what we did," I said.

"Yea, you right about that. Man, that nigga had to go. Once I saw that fuckin' video, I knew that was the end for him."

"Yea, me too. There was no way he could've gotten away with that shit!"

As we talked about that night, we recalled the night we went over to Dallas' place. That nigga had put up a good ass fight, but we were prepared for that shit. We choked his ass out because it was the easiest way to get him out of the house without causing any ruckus. The last thing we needed was to have the neighbors send the police before we had a chance to get the hell out.

Once we had him subdued, we tied him up with duct tape and threw him in the back of the truck. We headed to the bayou with rope and cinder blocks. We wrapped him up in tarp, tied the cinderblocks to him and tossed him in the water. The blocks held for a while, not as long as we had hoped though. Shit, we wanted him to disintegrate at the bottom of that bayou. But by the time he came up, all the evidence was gone so it didn't matter anyway.

No one knew that we were the ones who had murked that nigga. But he couldn't get away with what he did to Tangi. She was the love of my life and I knew that if we didn't kill him, he'd never leave her alone. He had to go.

Do I have regrets about killing Dallas? Nope, because someone had to do it. Did I have regrets about killing someone? Yes, because I wasn't that kind of man. I didn't go around killing people. But to save and protect my family, I'd do it again.

Any nigga who had a family would do the same thing I did to keep his family safe. For that, I had no regrets. Jay and I agreed that this was one secret we'd take to our graves. As long as Tangi and Sam was safe, it was all worth it and I hope that Dallas and his crazy ass mom are rotting in hell for the shit they put those women through.

Now we could all live in peace. *Good riddance!*

SURPRISE!! THE FINALE IS RIGHT AROUND THE CORNER...